ECHOES BENEATH

A Project Enterprise Story

PAULINE BAIRD JONES

Echoes Beneath

A PROJECT ENTERPRISE SHORT STORY

A routine mission turns into a planetary crisis.

Geologist Miles Walker travels to a remote world to inspect an old seismic sensor. He finds unexplained tremors, missing research, and Lira, an archaeologist searching for her missing father.

When a major quake reveals signs of an ancient alien presence, the danger escalates fast. Systems fail, sabotage surfaces, and something powerful begins to stir beneath the planet's crust. Lira's loyal and very opinionated space bird, T'Korrin, is the first to sense the threat.

Miles and Lira must combine science, courage, and trust to stop a disaster that could destroy more than one world. Falling for each other only raises the stakes.

Echoes Beneath is a science fiction romance adventure in the Project Enterprise universe, filled with alien secrets, high stakes danger, and heart.

Echoes Beneath first appeared in Pets in Space 10.

Echoes Beneath

"And why am I the one who needs to go check on him?" Lira Taan shoved a hand through her hair, barely resisting the urge to pull on it. What she really wanted to do was pull her brother's hair out, not her own.

There was a short silence on the other end while her brother tried to find a diplomatic way of saying he didn't want to go because it would make him crazy and besides, he had important things to do.

"Your work is more flexible," he finally said.

Lira had a feeling his wife had fed him that line. It was true. She was currently working from home compiling the data from her field work. Still, taking the time to fly down to the southern pole where their father lived hadn't been factored into her schedule.

"What about calling him?" Lira asked.

"I tried that. He told me he couldn't talk."

That was never a good sign.

"He told Keyvn he was close to first contact."

"With who?" Or was it whom? She always had to look it up and then she still wasn't sure. And whom sounded pretentious.

"Aliens."

Lira blinked. "*Aliens.*"

This wasn't exactly a surprise. Her father had managed to not just isolate himself at the southern pole of the planet, he'd alienated—bit of irony there—all his colleagues with his theories about ancient alien ruins hidden beneath the surface of Arroxan Prime. He believed there were multiple alien incursions, but until now he hadn't had any proof. And now he was claiming he'd had first contact?

Could anyone have contact with an ancient alien species? Didn't ancient imply long gone?

Lira sighed. Maybe they should have tried harder to persuade him not to move to the southern pole. However, it was a universal truth that parents never listened to their kids. If she had kids, she absolutely planned to not listen to them. It felt like she'd earned the privilege.

"You're closer," her brother said, his tone coaxing now. "Just pop down and make sure he's eating and stuff. Kevyn said he was acting a little erratic."

That was troubling. Her father was an odd mix of eccentric and grounded. Erratic? No.

She sighed again, knowing she would do it. As the only daughter, it was somehow her job to look after their father, to make sure he survived his various interesting life choices. And now that she let herself think about seeing him, she realized how much she did miss him. He was definitely quirky and often frustrating, but he was also a lot of fun. She couldn't explain how but being around him made her feel more centered somehow. The trouble was getting there. It was a pain.

The research facility where he lived hadn't started out as conspiracy theory central. It had originally been a weather tracking station. Her father had gotten a real deal on it—something they only heard about after it was too late to stop him. Though she had to admit, for a weather station, it had been a good deal. And it was interesting in a vaguely creepy kind of way. Now that she thought about it, it did have that weird alien vibe. Maybe that's why her father had gone all alien in his theories while living there mostly alone.

Early in his career, some funding had flowed his way, because he had started out researching seismic activity and how it might impact weather. Or be impacted by weather? Lira wasn't sure which and she had no idea why he'd moved on to aliens causing it or something like that. She'd been busy getting her archaeology degree and didn't know all the details from when he'd gone off the rails.

Sanity might have returned to her father when the funding dried up, but apparently conspiracy theories were catching. His funding now flowed from a variety of like-minded conspiracy theorists. It was too bad one of them didn't have to go down and make sure he was eating. And then there were his attempts to confirm his theory. She should probably make sure he wasn't going to doom them all to some kind of cataclysmic event.

It was challenging enough living with the current level of Arroxan Prime's seismic activity. It rendered parts of the planet uninhabitable and the rest interesting to inhabit. But it wasn't as if they had anywhere else to go. If scientists were to be believed, the other planets in their solar system were even less habitable. So, they'd learned to make do with what they had.

"All right," she said, when her brother let the silence apply pressure for the guilt trip. At least she'd get to pack for it before she left. "I'll go see what I can find out."

Her brother rang off without asking to be kept informed. Like she planned to let him off *that* hook. In some ways, he was as delusional as their father.

She looked at T'Korrin, her pet raptor. It fluffed its tiny wings in what looked like a shrug, then gave a tiny squawk. The look in his eyes was one she was familiar with.

"Don't you start," she said.

DR. MILES WALKER watched the runner lift off with something like relief. The pilot had been chatty in an obvious and annoying way. He also thought he was funny.

Yes, it was a bleak spot to be dropped off.

Yes, it was cold enough for him.

Probably a lot of rocks under that ice. Certainly enough rocks.

The hearty laugh followed these pieces of witticism.

The rock jokes were always the same, no matter which alien planet he was on. Of course there were enough rocks for him, more than enough rocks because planets they could land on were usually made of rocks.

No one ever asked him why rocks. Or why anyone cared about rocks. Or why send a geologist to look at the rocks of a planet without space capability. (He would like the answer to that question, too.)

They didn't need to ask. The questions were in their expressions and their voices. Since he couldn't, or didn't want to answer those questions, he was happy they didn't ask.

It wasn't, as he liked to tell people, rock science. It was earth science. Of course, he'd have liked to point out that geology wasn't only about rocks, but that would lead to more chatting and painful rock jokes.

It wasn't that Miles was opposed to chatting or even chatting about rocks. It was just that chatting—particularly pointless chatting—and mentally processing data were incompatible actions. He had been sent to Arroxan Prime to determine why a seismic sensor had triggered.

An ancient seismic sensor planted on Arroxan Prime a long time ago, hence the ancient designation.

It made sense to send a geologist to check it out. Seismic was part of a geologist's jam and they were comfortable with time frames of plus or minus millions of years. It made dating problematic since he and his dates counted time differently. If he wasn't a million years late, he should be good, right? But the answer was usually no.

That didn't mean this mission wasn't a head scratcher. Why had the sensor gone off now? It had been rolling happily along since it had been installed, and it chose now to go off?

"I'll be back to pick you up in three days, doc," the

pilot said in his earpiece. "And if you get in trouble, just trigger your alert."

"Thank you," Miles said, instead of using one of several sarcastic remarks he'd have liked to say. Not a good plan to annoy your ride. It had only taken once for him to learn that particular lesson.

"This is a singularly inhospitable place," Harold said, its voice still slightly robotic. It was getting better at not being a robotic sounding robot, however.

Harold was officially there to assist, but in reality it had been sent along so that no one would need to feel guilty about dropping him on an alien planet even further from Earth than the rest of the Earth Expedition, and then leaving him on that planet—a planet with an unhappy seismic sensor that probably just needed a new battery.

He stared up at the retreating shuttle. The sight gave him mixed feelings. On the one hand, he was finally—mostly—alone for this field trip. But this alone felt suddenly extremely alone when he looked at the empty landscape around him.

"I believe there are other places on this planet that are quite nice," Miles observed, somewhat absently. He tried to mentally match his topside location with the underlying formations that the ship's sensors had managed to identify.

It wasn't perfect. All he could judge it by were his

experiences with geology on other planets, and of course, on Earth. But there were always those little differences trying to trip him up. While he'd found similarities with Earth geology, each planet had its own unique way of putting it all together.

In a four-hundred-mile radius, the only human-made identifying surface marker was the facility, which was currently just out of his sightline. It had been deemed prudent to set him, Harold, and their gear down out of sight of the abandoned facility.

Miles found that ironic. If it was empty, what did it matter where they landed? At least they'd given them a surface runner to carry them and their equipment to the empty facility.

He knew beyond the rising peaks was a stratovolcano, or a composite volcano, if he'd translated the Garradian data correctly. From the air, it had had the appearance of one. It definitely had the conical shape and steep profile. He'd have liked to do a flyover of it, but it wasn't on their flight path. Maybe on the way out.

For now, his mission brief—aka field trip—appeared to be simple. The appearance of simple might worry him because geology was much more complicated than people realized. Still, it was nice to be dirt-side somewhere. A geologist wasn't that much use in outer space.

The Garradians, they seemed to do well in space now that they were back from what they called their long sleep. Apparently, they hadn't defrosted a geologist yet because the sensor activating had caught them off guard.

"It's probably a symptom of age," one non-geologist told him. Miles noticed he avoided making eye contact with him.

"Or its power source is almost expended," said another, equally evasive Garradian scientist.

Miles should probably have declined the honor of what could be the equivalent of changing a battery, but it was an alien planet full of unknown rocks. And it was probably safer than that time when he and some other geology students had rented a helicopter to fly over an erupting volcano.

And he hadn't had to pay anything for this ride. They were paying him.

They didn't have a lot of data, a fact that distressed the Garradians more than it did him. He just hated paperwork and dealing with it must have been at least as bad back whenever the sensor had been installed. And there was the language problem to factor in.

The Garradians managed communication on most things pretty well, considering how far apart their two cultures were, but the science stuff, the names? When two scientists of the same persuasion were together, they could mostly find their way to common ground.

But he'd had to spend the trip trying to find anything he recognized in the data provided without context or a counterpart. For an alien planet in another galaxy.

The only thing the Garradians seemed certain of was that the sensor going off was more than troubling. He'd deduced this because they'd repeated "troubling" multiple times. In fact, that was almost the last word they'd said to him just before he boarded his ride.

"It is troubling."

He'd wanted to ask them if it was troubling, just to yank their chains, but a look from General Halliwell had stopped him.

Harold's onboard AI had been able to help with some things.

The planet's inhabitants called it Arroxan Prime.

It was a heavily volcanic planet with limited livable space.

The sensor had been located at the planet's southern pole.

It was an ice pole, but with volcanos in close enough proximity to be a possible reason the sensor had triggered. Even though the pole and the volcano had been in close proximity for pretty much the whole time.

What didn't he know?

Why they were so worried enough about seismic activity in a place without inhabitants that they placed a sensor—or multiple sensors—in that particular location? Was it actually a seismic sensor? But what else could it be?

That was a pretty big knowledge gap. He knew all about big gaps. Canyons, ravines, crevasses lurking under the ice waiting for an unwary geologist to fall into.

Their first task on arriving in orbit at Arroxan Prime had been to initiate scanning protocols to get updated information both on the sensor and the planet as a whole. He rolled his eyes again as he considered this. If the sensor could be accessed and rebooted without a landing, that was the preferred option.

If he was unable to adequately determine the problem, then his rules of engagement allowed for he and Harold to go dirt side as long as they didn't make contact with the inhabitants.

Arroxan Prime's population weren't space capable.

First contact was tricky and he wasn't qualified to do it.

Well, he couldn't argue with that. He wasn't that great at first contact with other Earthlings. So he was anxious to avoid any contact with the inhabitants, too. And he was pretty sure they didn't want to talk to him.

Being recruited to the Expedition had changed his perception of first contact.

Prior to that, his "contacts" with aliens was via movies, television, and books. Fictional contact without risk. He knew it was ironic when he routinely went down mines and liked looking down the mouths of volcanos. But no one had required him to make sense until he left Earth to join the expedition.

And honestly, since then, not much had made sense. Like lava, he just went with the flow.

And that had landed him here on Arroxan Prime with a robot for a sidekick. Now there was some irony.

What he thought he knew, after his study and the scanning, was that the sensor was deep underground. And that some kind of facility sat directly on top of it. And what he knew for sure was that he couldn't reset it from space or figure out why it had triggered.

He was less sure of a few things, but he thought the geologist equivalent Garradians of the past had installed some kind of barrier down there and left sensors to monitor it. He hadn't been able to figure out why.

That was odd, ranging to downright weird. The only reason to install a barrier was to keep things down, but the minerals deep down in most planets just found another way to the surface if that was where it wanted to go.

When man—or humanoids—went head-to-head with Mother Nature? They usually lost when Mom brought all the things.

On the other hand, whatever they'd done appeared to have lasted for Miles' plus or minus a millennia. So, it was a good effort.

And hopefully all he'd need to do was to change a battery. Harold also had a program update if the equipment they'd left there was still functional. That seemed like the longest of the long shots. But he had to like their optimism.

Even if it was his geological butt on the line.

Their scans had shown no life signs in or around the facility. Looking around? This wasn't a surprise. And it was good since this was **not** a first contact mission. Just in case he'd missed the memo the first fifteen times.

And even though it wasn't a first contact mission, they'd loaded both his suit systems and Harold's memory banks with everything that was known about Arroxan Prime and its inhabitants, including any language variations that may have occurred since they were last there.

There weren't as many of those as he'd have expected for a whole world, but their flyover and scan had confirmed the fact that most of the planet was uninhabitable. Harold had used some of the scanning time to update the databases with what could be retrieved from Arroxan Prime's communications. They didn't seem to have any satellites. Not a surprise since they weren't space capable, yet somehow he was still surprised. They did have airborne type transportation systems, more even than Earth.

So they clearly had the capability to be space capable.

But when he saw how often the planet experienced seismic events, it did kind of make sense. Putting fuel in a rocket ship on an unstable surface might not be the best idea.

When he'd asked why it felt like they didn't want first contact but had still given him all the information he'd need if he did, someone called Doc had told him to expect the unexpected.

"I'm a geologist," he'd told her. "We never expect the expected."

He remembered her grin sent a chill down his back. That was one scary lady.

He supposed it was a lucky break that the source of the signal came from this unpromising and remote location. He tried not to remind himself that luck could go both ways.

He might have wished his ride didn't have to pop off to pick up some botanists or something from a Mars-like planet on the other side of the system. It would have been nice to know it was orbiting overhead and ready for a quick pick up if something went wrong.

His ride had been equipped with a lot of high-end, Garradian equipment, so the scans they'd done prior to this drop had provided him with a butt load of data, but he'd still been left without the kind of conclusive data that could only be secured by coming down and taking a look.

He liked to look, even knowing that most of what he'd like to see was inaccessible to his eyes. He did have a built-in Lidar along with some other stuff in his suit systems that he hoped would help him collect the necessary data. And he had his rock pick. He might have smuggled that on board. The Garradians didn't seem to like pointy ended hammers. Weird.

Being able to use his rock pick to collect some new rocks was definitely the upside of the mission.

He looked around. The cold? He didn't like that as much.

At least the Garradian gear was top notch and pretty cool to wear. The only actual chill was from being almost alone on the alien planet with a robot called Harold. Who named a robot Harold? he'd asked.

It had chosen the name itself, he'd been told. So, Harold it was.

They'd pitched the idea of Harold by using Miles' love of sci-fi stuff against him.

"You'll be like Luke," they said.

They hadn't completely misled him. He had a ray gun instead of a light saber and a 3CPO-like robot that called itself Harold. So far Harold hadn't tried to give him protocol lessons. That was a positive.

He might have objected to the prissy robot, but they had given him a weapons load out, too. They couldn't send him down here without some way to defend himself, presumably from an ice flow because he was under no circumstances to make contact with anyone. The "don't shoot anyone" didn't have to be said out loud, because that came under the heading of first contact, too.

If there were some kind of ice creature living here? It hadn't shown up on their scans. So, it was probably fine.

"Let's get going," he said. At least they didn't have to walk the rest of the way, thanks to the small land runner. That was pretty *Star Wars* cool, too.

Harold slid into the driving side. Miles didn't object. He'd never driven a runner on an icy surface, and it would be embarrassing to screw up in front of a robot. And he liked to look around, which was something one shouldn't do while driving.

As they started forward, he continued trying to mentally place them with what he'd seen from above. They were on the edge of a plain that spread across a valley almost completely surrounded by jagged rocky peaks. Okay, they were probably rock. They could be completely ice formations. Good thing he'd brought a rock pick.

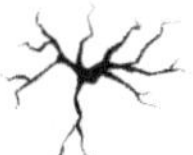

LIRA STEERED the air flyer between the soaring and jagged peaks that surrounded her father's research facility. It was as bleak and cheerless a spot as anything on Arroxan Prime—and there was a lot of bleak and inhospitable to choose from. Her brothers thought it was crazy. Her father considered this a major positive. No one could just drop in for a visit.

He liked to know who was incoming. Sometimes that was so he could pretend he wasn't there. Her father wasn't what you'd call a people person, but if she wound him up just right, he told great stories. He distrusted the government and he tended to latch onto theories and ride them to a crash point. The alien obsession had lasted a little longer than most, though all of them eventually looped back to the seismic disruptions Arroxan Prime experienced with disconcerting irregularity.

Her father believed in a long-term solution. He'd always been a solutions-oriented dreamer.

Over time, their people had adapted to the disruptions. They hadn't had another choice. Her dad wasn't the only one looking for answers. Most of their scientists spent a lot of time either trying to figure out how to stop the persistent and irregular tremors, or how to more effectively live with them.

So far, the "learn to live with them" track was winning the study war. Their buildings were now constructed on specialized pressure plates designed to absorb the movement, they'd been built using flexible components, their personal items weren't breakable, and they all had learned how to walk with that movement and not against it. Face planting was a good teacher.

Ground transportation was rare because it got old fixing roads over and over again.

Her father was firmly in the fix-it camp, even with the divergence into alien conspiracy. If the aliens did it, then the solution to fix it was there, just waiting to be found. Problem solved. The possible first contact with aliens was new, though.

At least he'd taken her call and was happy for her to visit. He had sounded odd, however. A new odd, instead of his regular odd.

She made a small course adjustment as more of the plain came into view. Crouched on the plain that lapped up against the mountains, the facility had been constructed almost dead center. Just visible between two of those peaks, she saw their southern moon. There were also theories about it, and their northern moon, and the moons' gravitational effect on planetary seismic activity. There were indications in the archaeological record that their ancestors had believed the moons were responsible.

Lira couldn't say she kept up with the current theories. Her interest was the past. It was fascinating to study the signs of previous inhabitants and also discover the innovative ways they'd dealt with the tremors. The seismic disruptions had been a problem for a long time.

T'Korrin made a disgruntled noise from where he crouched under the passenger seat. He was an odd bird for sure. He had to go everywhere she went, or he made himself sick, but he also didn't like flying. Even under his own steam.

A bird who didn't like to fly.

When she'd told him where she was going, he'd hopped from leg to leg making agitated noises before finally deciding it would be worse to be left behind. He'd also made his displeasure known for most of the trip. She didn't know how he did it, but he managed to sound like a whining two-year-old.

She postulated that it was because he'd been orphaned young. She'd found him on a dig, his parents likely killed or kidnapped by poachers. He'd bonded to her at first sight. When he wasn't whining, he was adorable. He was also a wonderful sensor. He gave almost early warnings of incoming tremors. She might wish he'd do it a little sooner, but any warning was good.

She'd tried to teach him how to fly, but it wasn't like she could show him. He had a way of looking at her when she tried to get him to use his wings that was… disconcerting. She always felt like she was the one who didn't get it.

If she sometimes suspected he could fly? Well, so far, she hadn't been able to catch him at it.

He blinked up at her, a soulful look in his deep, dark predator's eyes.

"We're almost there," she told him.

The locater beam for incoming visitors to her father's facility activated and she adjusted course. The landing pad was in front of the facility. She squinted at the entrance. Was there something parked there?

She positioned her flyer over the pad and began her descent, pausing as T'Korrin gave his signature "tremor incoming" squeak. She delayed touchdown as the landscape rippled and swayed.

"That was a rather long one," she told T'Korrin when she was finally able to land.

There'd be aftershocks, but anyone who grew up on Arroxan Prime knew how to deal.

Now that she was dirtside, she could see there was definitely some kind of craft right up next to the entrance. Of course, her father needed to get supplies from time to time. The facility had some self-sustaining features, but he did need stuff. She was always happy when the available food wasn't just facility grown.

She did wonder why they'd parked there and not on the landing pad. Stuff to unload perhaps?

She waited for T'Korrin to jump onto her shoulder and then scrambled out onto the icy surface of the landing pad. She paused to get her balance as the smaller tremors continued to ripple through the ground, their impact somewhat mitigated by the pad's design.

Usually she recognized most types of flyer. She'd been in most of them going to and from dig sites, but this one was new to her. A new type, perhaps?

Balance secured, she headed toward the flyer and the facility. It was a two-seater, with rear space where she saw cargo containers. A supply run? It could be, she supposed. But lines were awfully sleek for cargo hauler. It had a symbol on one side that she didn't recognize. She traced it with a finger.

"What do you think, T'Korrin?"

He squawked and jumped to its roof, walking

around it as if examining it. She crossed her arms and grinned. When he jumped back to her shoulder, she met his gaze.

"Well?" She would swear he shrugged. "Well, let's go find my father."

IT WAS AN ODD PLACE, Miles thought as he hesitated in the entryway. From the outside, it looked like a government standard facility. Gray, boring, ugly. Inside, there were signs of intelligent design. Light flooded down from slits in the ceiling. Natural light? It's what it seemed to be.

The entrance was what he'd have called a small rotunda because he liked to think funny words and rotunda was definitely on the list. The decoration wasn't inspired, but it looked like someone had tried, not very hard, but trying was trying.

The floor was plain except for the crack cutting from one side of the little rotunda to another

"That crack propagated like it had a grudge." He glanced at Harold and then sighed. A sidekick with no sense of humor.

"No crevasse though." It was always better if there weren't crevasses in your path.

Two doorways led off from both sides, but when he checked one, they came together again in a short, single hallway.

Interesting.

More cracks in the walls and the next—it wasn't a rotunda, but it was round. An atrium? He studied the plants on the other side, looking through a series of fine cracks and impact stars in the glass. Was it glass? He touched it, but of course, his gloves didn't provide the kind of tactile experience he needed.

There was an acceptable atmosphere, according to his Garradian gear, so he pulled off a glove and tried again.

It wasn't glass. He might have been surprised, but then he recalled the planet's seismic activity and reconsidered. It was probably the smart move when the ground could move at any time.

Had they abandoned this facility after a seismic event? He lowered his faceplate and inhaled carefully. He couldn't define what he smelled, but it wasn't what he'd experienced in abandoned buildings back on Earth.

The plants were still growing inside the atrium, too.

"We're sure no one lives here?" he asked Harold.

"There is no way to be certain no one lives here," it said. "We detected no life signs."

The careful parsing made him turn to look at Harold, but it couldn't break out in expression.

He wished they didn't have to enter this building, abandoned temporarily or not. But the Garradian signal was coming from somewhere directly under it. And traversing a building was probably better than trying to dig a hole in the ice crust.

He could admit to curiosity to see this sensor—if that would be possible. No way to tell how deep this facility went, but according to his suit's reading, they were still significantly above the signal.

Past the atrium, they found a couple of offices and then some living quarters. One definitely looked occupied. Miles didn't say anything about it. Just shut the door and moved on, hoping that the life signs scan was right and there was no one here. Or someone would be returning soon?

"We might need to work fast," he muttered. And how would that affect our pickup time? They'd planned on camping out here until their ride came back in a few days.

He glanced around. His overall impression of what he'd seen so far was that the bureaucratic mind-set was inter-galactic.

He'd initially assumed that the facility had been installed to study the seismic in the area. The proximity of stratovolcano made that likely, but now that they'd reached the research area, he wasn't so sure.

He studied some charts pinned to the walls.

"These are weather data," Harold said, coming to stand next to him.

It wasn't totally crazy. Earth had weather stations in a lot of unlikely places. It did feel like they'd missed the obvious.

He ran a finger along a desktop and then studied the dust it had collected. He looked back. Their footprints were clearly visible on the floor entering this room. So whoever was living here, they didn't come in here.

He picked up a cup and looked at the gunk crusted inside. If he had to guess—which he did—he'd guess it was made of a similar material as the glass on the atrium. He checked out other items. They were all unbreakable. He dropped a small object whose purpose he couldn't figure out. It bounced.

As if in response to his action, a tremor began, small at first, then building. He grabbed the side of the desk to steady himself and realized it was bolted down.

When the tremor subsided, Harold picked up the object and studied it briefly before returning it to its spot on the desk. It was easy to find, thanks to the dust circle.

"This structure absorbs some of the instability of

the tremor," Harold said. "My system registered a much higher event than we felt."

"That would be worth knowing about," Miles said. It made sense that the people of Arroxan Prime had adapted their buildings, not just their travel, to life with a lot of seismic activity. Scientists on Earth had made progress in factoring in stress during building construction but this seemed next level. Though it didn't always work. He thought about the cracks they'd observed along the way.

If he had to guess, which he did, and as a geologist, mostly had to do, he'd say the building had experienced a major seismic event fairly recently. It might be why the facility had been abandoned, or mostly abandoned. Or recently abandoned?

"There is a handwritten note on this chart," Harold said.

Miles looked over his shoulder, and saw it standing in front of the chart directly behind the desk.

"What does it say?" He leaned in, but the writing might as well have been his doctor's on a prescription.

"This is wrong."

"Okay." He glanced around, but there were no rocks in this room. Time to move on.

Back out in the hallway, he realized what he'd been feeling without thinking it. It was all kind of retro, like a 50s sci-fi movie. Even though the light distribution from the ceiling slits was pretty good, it still felt a bit murky. Or maybe it was unease with the shadows in the corners where the light didn't reach.

He turned and flashed a light into one corner. Nothing moved and he felt stupid.

"Did you hear something?" Harold asked.

"No."

"A human intuition?" Harold sounded curious and not judgy.

"I feel like we're being watched, which is probably imagination, not intuition."

"You are probably correct," Harold said.

He'd brought it on himself, but that didn't help contain the spike of annoyance.

"Is there any way to tap into systems here and get access to local data?" He probably wouldn't be able to figure it out any better than the Garradian data, but it was a good deflection.

For what felt like a long slow moment, Harold studied him. Finally, it appeared to blink. "I am not picking up wireless transmissions. I will require a port for access."

Miles waved at the systems bank inside the room next to where they stood. "What about one of those?"

"They aren't powered." Harold turned and left.

Miles followed him out the door but by the time

he'd reached the hallway, Harold was no longer in sight. Dude could move when it wanted to.

He didn't like being left alone, but he also didn't want to hurry after Harold. He reached a small junction of hallways and realized he might not be able to hurry after Harold.

The silence added to the overall creepy vibes he was trying not to notice.

For something to do, he checked the signal, turning to find its direction, and headed down that hall. It wasn't a long one. He tried a door and found a staircase. He checked the signal again. He was almost standing right on top of it. But it was still far below.

If the hallway was creepy, the stairs were next level. They curved out of sight into a murky, gray gloom. He castigated himself to get moving and went down the steps but at the bend, found a rubble fall. He didn't mind retreating back up the stairs, but he did bend to grab a couple of smaller samples from the rubble.

As the door swung shut behind him, he thought he heard something. Harold? He angled his head to listen, but it wasn't repeated. Probably Harold, he told himself. Had to be Harold. No life signs, remember?

He started back the way he'd come and felt his skin prickle. He usually didn't let his imagination get this out of control.

Just because this place had creepy alien vibes, didn't mean it had creepy aliens inhabiting it.

Life signs. What did that actually mean? The people of Arroxan Prime were humanoid, he'd been told. So surely the life signs scanners could pick them up. But…

He gave a shake of his shoulders. It was a bit like being in almost every sci-fi movie he'd ever seen. Well, not every one of them. Just the creepy ones. His gaze tracked around, then moved up to eye the vents. He kind of wished he hadn't lost track of Harold. And then he heard a noise again. Man, he hoped that was Harold.

THE OUTSIDE DOOR had been left partly ajar, igniting a sense of unease that only intensified as Lira eased through the gap, not sure why she didn't want to push the door further open. It did squeak, but that shouldn't matter. Even knowing this, she paused, folded her head gear back, and then paused and listened.

The deep, brooding silence raised the hair on the back of her neck for no reason she could define.

Since her father lived here alone, there weren't usually overt signs of habitation, but there were usually some. And he did have a way of making his presence felt, even if it was just the smell of some food cooking.

When she started to step forward, T'Korrin made a noise. He jumped down from her shoulder and clicked his way to something she hadn't seen before.

A long crack in the floor.

"You're right," she said. "That's new." And troubling. As old as the facility was, her father had insisted that the stress-reducing system was adequate to the task.

She opened her mouth to call out and then…didn't.

Pale light came in from slits that had been tucked into the ceilings to keep the light from being direct. It had something to do with orbits and how this place faced the sun. It wasn't a fact she'd needed to keep hold of, so she hadn't.

The silence seemed to expand and grow until it almost felt alive. Even T'Korrin jumped back onto her shoulder and shrank against her, trying to make himself smaller. His small whimper was only audible to her.

She pulled out her weapon and set it to stun, even while chiding herself for letting the atmosphere get to her.

Aliens.

Her brother could have been tweaking her with that. It felt like guys never quite grew out of the urge to tease. But she didn't put her weapon away as she paced forward. Even in the low light, she knew her way around the facility, so she didn't hesitate…much.

It would serve her father right if she accidentally stunned him. She sighed, knowing she didn't mean it and it was very like him to get lost in his research and forget she was coming. She just wished she knew why it felt…hostile…for the first time in her experience in coming here.

This wasn't her first time venturing into a possibly hostile space. On remote digs, there was always a chance of running into site robbers. This was the first time unease had prickled down her back like ice in this place, however. This was her father's place. It usually felt safe.

There was more damage to the garden containment. She touched the place where cracks spread out in a star pattern and bit her lip, but she didn't speak this time.

At an intersection, she paused to check the side corridors and listen.

Still nothing to hear.

Where was her father? And where was whoever had arrived on that flyer? Granted, she'd never been here when her father had guests, so she didn't know what that sounded like. Or where he took them.

She continued forward, while unease continued its rise inside her. She probably shouldn't have watched that spooky movie last night. If this were that movie, which would she be? The disposable character or the heroine who gets to live…but was forever traumatized by events?

She heard a slight sound and frowned. It kind of sounded like a system coming online. Yes, there was a beep. She followed the sound with her weapon ready. A door up ahead was open. She paced forward and peered around the corner and saw…

She didn't know what she saw. She half lowered her weapon as she stared. What in seven stars was it?

It was humanoid in shape but clearly made of some kind of metal alloy. It was tall, much taller than she was, laying a shadow across the floor that stretched to and partly up the wall. She knew her jaw had dropped, and she couldn't seem to close it as more of the instrument panels hummed into life, lights flickering across the various screens, buttons flashing and igniting little points of light over the surface of the…alien? Was this her father's first contact?

It shifted and light gleamed on metal. It looked a bit like a robot. That was almost a relief. She wasn't sure why it was easier to consider than an alien. She hadn't realized robotic science had gotten this far.

She thought it spoke, though the only word she caught was the word "Walker."

Walker? What did that even mean?

When she didn't respond, the head of the creature turned—not the body—just the head. It stared at her, its eyes changing color twice, not unlike the lights on a data system.

"Oh," it said. There might have been a humming sound. She wasn't sure, but when it spoke this time, she understood it.

"You're not Doctor Walker. That's most unfortunate."

Walker was a name? Lira lifted her weapon again. "How?"

There were more questions, but all she was able to produce was the single word. Now its body turned, though not completely. It appeared to be tethered by a wire of some kind. It was attached to a port in a panel. It lifted its hands.

"I am not going to hurt you. I'm programmed to protect human life."

She half lowered the weapon again, not sure she felt comforted by this statement or more freaked out. "You're a…"

"I am a robot. My name is Harold."

A robot. A robotic humanoid. Again, not a field of

research she'd looked into, though she'd been on teams that used drones for dangerous explorations. Maybe she should keep better track of what was happening outside her fields of interest.

"Did my father…build you?" He must have, unless the robot had arrived in that flyer outside. She frowned. Had it driven the flyer? That actually made more sense than her father suddenly becoming a roboticist. But a robot driving a flyer? Did that make sense? She tensed. Was it alone? No, she reminded herself. Somewhere here there was this Voss person? Thing?

"No."

Harold seemed quite definite about that.

"Did you and," she hesitated, "the Walker person… arrive on that flyer outside?"

"Yes."

"To meet with my father?"

Something about the look in its eyes made her think it was trying to process her question. Finally, it spoke.

"No."

Only this time it didn't sound that certain.

She heard the scuff of a footfall and spun around, her weapon coming up again.

A man stood there, an actual human man, half in gloom, half in pale light, his hands also lifted.

"Oh dear," he said.

MILES STUDIED THE WOMAN, trying to figure out what to say, what to do.

Don't make first contact, they'd said and now here he was, making first contact, or was it second contact since she'd been talking to Harold? Was it a loophole he could use? That it was Harold's fault?

"This is," Harold began and then stopped. "I don't know your name."

Miles blinked and then realized Harold was talking about the woman. He looked at her. She studied him the same way he looked at a rock sample. He wasn't sure he liked it. Of course, he wasn't a rock.

Like him, she wore what appeared to be gear designed for the weather, but she had a bird sitting on her shoulder. It was a pugnacious looking bird, white, with feathers standing up around its little head and a beak that looked like it would be able to do some damage some day. A band of orange gave its eyes a bandit look and its expression kind of mirrored the woman's. It felt a little rude.

"I am Lira Taan."

The translation program in his suit was pretty effective. The pause was almost unnoticeable. *Lira Taan.* That was probably a name.

"Miles Walker," he said. *Lira.* The name suited her, he decided. She had what he'd call practical good looks. She was medium height, with a sturdy build, and her brown hair was pulled away from strong, clean features. Her green gaze was both clear and direct. He wished she wasn't still pointing her weapon at him, but other than that, he liked what he saw.

He was pretty sure she wasn't reciprocating that feeling.

"Are you here to see my father?"

Her tone remained suspicious. Clearly, she was also intelligent. Their presence here was suspicious, he reminded himself, even as he tried to come to terms with her father living here. If her father lived here, why had they registered no life signs?

"Your father?" He repeated her words to stall for time. It didn't help. He glanced around him. "I haven't seen anyone since we got here. Have you seen anyone, Harold?"

"No."

The look she gave him was one he totally deserved.

"So, you just walked in?"

"The door wasn't locked." Her brows arched and he added, "There's not really anywhere else to go around here, is there?"

Her lips quirked slightly, and he gave her a hopeful smile.

"Fair point." She glanced around now, somewhat uneasily, he thought. "I'm surprised he hasn't heard us." Her gaze tracked to Harold. "Are you a roboticist, Dr. Walker, was it?"

The bird made an odd sound.

"I'm a geologist," he said. Had that word translated correctly? As if to help him out, a tremor started, making him stagger once before he managed to catch his balance. He noticed she rode it out like a champ. That was some good balance.

He waved a hand vaguely around. "I study seismic activity and stuff." He could have mentioned all the various geologic things he studied, but it all seemed moot now. And she hadn't yet asked him what they were doing here in a place where this was the only habitation.

"Oh. Interesting," she said.

Was it? She didn't sound interested.

She hesitated for another long moment, then stowed her weapon. "My father is usually in one of the old labs. It is this way."

As she passed him, he caught a whiff of something clean, something planet-bound from her. He'd missed planet type smells, he realized. She moved smoothly, confidently ahead of them. He exchanged a look with Harold, who shrugged and pointed to the connection between it and the computer.

"Catch up when you can," he said, and headed after Lira.

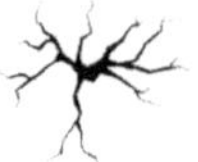

THERE WAS something different about him, Lira mused as she walked with his footsteps padding after her. She might be surprised she'd let him follow her. Turning her back on a stranger wasn't the brightest move, but she sensed that he was as uneasy as she was with their meeting. If they hadn't come to see her father, why were they here? And why didn't she just ask him that? Why didn't she want to know?

She kind of, Lira admitted, liked the look of him. His brown eyes were a bit vague, as if his mind were on other things, but they were also…kind. It almost made her smile, because his eco-suit was trim and fitted, but she still had the feeling that he was normally rumpled. In fact, he reminded her a bit of her father who was the original rumpled man.

She almost sighed then. Her father was brilliant, absent-minded, distracted by multiple ideas until he'd locked onto something and then he was unrelenting. Her father was also kind when he remembered and as chaotic as the seismic disturbances he so desperately wanted to understand.

He was also very hard to live with. And very hard to live without, she added with a slight smile. Her steps quickened some at the thought of seeing him again. He'd stare at her for a moment, his gaze unfocused, then his eyes would light up and his arms would go out. The welcome hug was the best.

She'd arrived like a mother—or possibly like *her* mother—to deal with a recalcitrant elder and instead of an elder, she felt reduced to child status. Maybe that was the real reason her brothers didn't like to do this.

He had charm, her father did, or something better than charm, perhaps. But her heart quickened at the idea of seeing him. It had been too long. How easy it was to let the days slip away, to get locked into thinking she was too old to need him and then just like that, she was desperate to see him.

She wanted to hear him talk about what he was working on, even if it was about aliens. And she really wanted to hear about the earthquake that had caused so much damage. There were signs of it everywhere. Cracks running up the walls and across the floors. Some signs of rubble in the rooms. Thankfully the hallway was still clear, though there seemed to be a lot of dust being stirred up by their passage.

He'd set up in one of the smaller labs toward the back of the facility. The equipment he'd set up always puzzled her, too, but again, not her area of scientific expertise. The door was ajar and T'Korrin jumped off her shoulder and ran forward. He loved her father, a fact that puzzled them both. Maybe what T'Korrin really loved was annoying him by loving him. In some ways he was like a cat, latching on to the one person in the room who didn't like cats.

By the time Lira reached the door and pulled it wider, T'Korrin was drooping on a tabletop. The bird did sad very well. He gave a mournful chirp.

"He's not here?" She tried to hide her dismay from the stranger. *Miles Walker*. She knew T'Korrin wasn't wrong. She could feel the emptiness of the room, but she walked forward anyway, looking for signs of… something.

There was damage in here, she noted, but none of the equipment could be damaged unless something fell on top of it and then it usually could be repaired. They made everything very resilient.

Dr. Walker followed her in, but he headed directly toward a table covered with rock samples.

That was new.

She had to admit it was kind of…cute the way he picked up and studied each sample. At one point he pulled out a small device and used it to study a rock. Then he began to hum and sing. Something about a blueberry hill.

Harold made a sound and Dr. Walker looked up.

"You are singing," Harold said.

"I am?" Dr. Walker gave her an embarrassed smile. "Sorry."

"It's fine," she said. It had been kind of nice. She knew what thrill meant but what was a blueberry hill?

He resumed his study of the rocks. Clearly, they told him more than they did her. He picked up a white rock, one with facets. He turned it over in his hands and then held it to his mouth and licked it.

"Dr. Walker," she began.

He looked at her. "It's salt." He held it out to her.

"Do I have to lick it?" she asked, taking the sample.

He grinned and shook his head. "You can take my word for it."

That felt like a challenge. She licked her fingertip and lightly rubbed it on the rock, then tasted it.

"It is salt." She agreed with his assessment, though she didn't know why it mattered. He'd sounded surprised.

"Do you think your father collected these here?" He gestured vaguely around.

"Probably." She bent over. Each sample had been labeled. She vaguely recognized some of the names. *Crysalithe. Solvate. Ferrocryx.* Digs dealt with rock strata, too, but there was always an onsite strata scientist for that. She frowned.

The last time she'd been here, her father had still

been deep into volcanics. Some of these minerals were associated with volcanics, but the others were new to her. Next to the names were a series of numbers.

"What do the numbers mean?" Dr. Walker asked.

"Well, if this were an archeological site, those would be locations. We use a grid map to keep track of where we found things." She studied the numbers. The first number was usually a grid, then next the grid square, and the last would be a depth reading, if applicable.

She told him this and then looked around, still puzzled. Where was her father collecting samples from? The facility was enclosed and it was all ice outside, unless he got close to the volcano. And that was over the mountain range.

"Depths," Dr. Walker's voice was thoughtful.

She spotted a familiar notebook and went over and picked it up. Inside were her father's notes, but he used a kind of shorthand. He'd have a voice recorder, too, somewhere. She flipped a page and a folded sheet dropped out.

Dr. Walker picked it up and unfolded it, holding it so she could see it.

"It's a map," she said. "Well, a kind of map." It wasn't like the ones she used on digs. It was hand drawn for one thing.

"May I?" he asked. She nodded and he spread it on the table near the rock samples.

She watched him for a few minutes, then went back to studying the pages. Back when, she'd learned to read his shorthand, but it had been a while, and his handwriting had gotten worse.

She did recognize the dates. She flipped through the book until she got to their current date and then began to work her way back.

Three weeks ago, something had happened. His handwriting had gotten worse for one thing. She lifted the book closer. She couldn't be sure and yet…she had a feeling that there'd been a big tremor. She turned a page and found a small drawing. It looked like a ball, or part of one.

She noticed that Dr. Walker had looked up and was looking around him, then he'd look at the map again as if trying to orient himself. Then he'd pick up a rock and study it.

She edged over and looked down at the map. It had to be connected to the notebook somehow. Maybe her father had sketched out the epicenter of the earthquake?

"There are numbers that seem to match up to some of the rocks," Dr. Walker said. "And then this," he pointed to what had appeared to be a list written on the edge, but it was also numbers, she saw.

He was frowning, the salt sample in his hand.

"Is something wrong, Dr. Walker?"

He looked up and then smiled. "Please call me Miles, ma'am."

Without conscious thought, she smiled back. "If you'll call me Lira." Ma'am? What was that all about?

"Deal," he said. Then he held up the salt but also picked up another rock. "This rock shouldn't be in close proximity to this salt, but if I'm reading this correctly, they were found together."

"Found where?"

"That's a good question. Is there another dig site?"

"That would require heavy equipment," she said. Her father couldn't afford as much light equipment as he'd like to have, let alone anything heavy.

"That's what I thought." Miles looked around him again.

Lira noticed he had another of the samples in his other hand, his fingers rubbing the surface. "Can I?" she asked. He held it out to her, and she took it. It was smooth. "That's not natural," she said. "I wonder where he found it."

"I was wondering the same thing," Miles said. "What's below?"

She half frowned. "Do you know something?"

He ran a hand through his hair and the frown

faded. "I know a lot of things. Not sure what's relevant to the situation though."

"I meant about my father."

"Oh, no. I don't know anything about him."

He sounded certain, but… "Then why are you here?"

Now he looked discomfited. "We picked up a sensor alarm, a seismic sensor, in this area."

She arched her brows. "Only one? There is a lot of seismic activity here." She glanced at the crack running down the wall behind him.

"This was a special alarm. A concerning alarm." He hesitated. "What's below?"

"As far as I know some shallow storage. It's not that easy to go deep here." Surely, he noticed all the ice outside.

"Can you show me?"

"Of course. I think there is access off the kitchen."

She led him out, T'Korrin hopping after them.

"Does your father spend a lot of time here?" Miles asked, his tone casual.

She looked at him. "He lives here." He really didn't know anything about her father.

"Oh." He paused. "Interesting."

Lira stopped and faced him, her hands on her hips. "Is there something going on that I should know about?"

Dr. Walker cleared his throat again. "I'm surprised anyone would live here."

Well, she couldn't blame him for that, or the look he cast around him.

"He's eccentric," Lira said. Her slight, wry grin earned her a very nice smile from Miles. A small shiver ran down her spine at the sight of it. The moment stretched out and then they both started at the sound of approaching footsteps. Harold came into view.

Was it her imagination that Miles now looked relieved?

Her brows creased, she resumed walking for a few more steps and pushed the kitchen door open. It was chaotic. Pans and dishes were all over the floor and covered with a layer of dust. Nothing was broken because they couldn't break, but it was a mess. There was a big crack in the ceiling and one of the refrigeration units had fallen forward.

"You should let us go first," Miles said.

"I will go first," Harold said.

"We should let Harold go first," Miles said. "He's very good at going first."

"All right," Lira said, repressing a smile. She wasn't sorry to let the robot go first, just in case there were bugs down there. Even in the southern pole there were crawling critters. "The storage room access is on the other side."

The robot picked its way forward, shifting debris aside with its feet, clearing a path for them to follow.

Miles set out after it and she followed him.

About halfway, Harold turned. “This facility is remarkably stable.”

What was remarkable about that? She glanced around at the chaos and wondered why it thought that. Then they reached the access door. A red light over it was flashing.

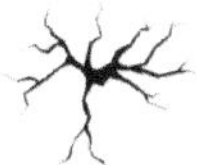

MILES STARED up at the red light.

“It doesn’t mean anything,” Lira said.

He looked at her.

“I mean, it means that,” she faltered, “that it’s been breached. The storage isn’t secure. But it’s not a real problem. Not really.”

Was that what it meant? Miles wasn’t so sure, but Harold didn’t seem to care. It reached for the handle and pulled the door open.

The puff of air held the scents of earth, some food going bad perhaps, and something he didn’t recognize. No, he did recognize it. *Salt.* It smelled like a salt flat. But, as he previously noted, salt formations and volcanics weren’t typically found together. That was true on Earth, of course and this wasn't Earth. But that had been consistent on the other planets he'd been asked to geologically assess.

And the sample that Lira had agreed with him hadn't been formed naturally? But if he was reading her father's notes correctly—which he might not be—both the salt and that sample had been collected at the same depth. Here somewhere.

Since he couldn't answer his own question, he stepped through the door after Harold and immediately had to duck his head. The low ceiling was heavily beamed and was definitely a basement. But the smell of salt flats was stronger here.

"Over here," Harold said.

Miles went to him but stopped at the sight of the jagged scar at the end of the room. A faint glow seemed to come from the hole. He stepped closer, kneeling to examine the edges. Harold gave him extra light to study several of the stones scattered on the floor.

He heard Lira join them.

"My father didn't mention that when I talked to him," she said, sounding resigned.

Miles looked up at her. "Do you think he went down there?"

"I don't want to think it," she said. "But it is likely that's where he is."

Lira sounded both resigned and unhappy. Miles felt relieved. Their seismic signal was down there, and he'd been wondering how they were going to reach it.

The bird came up to the edge of the hole and gazed down, then hopped out of sight.

"I guess we're going in," Miles said.

Harold lowered itself down into the hole and then looked back up at Miles. "There are stairs but there is also more debris."

"Stairs?" Lira rubbed her face. "Stairs."

He should have let the lady go first, but he wasn't sure that good manners worked the same in another galaxy when descending into an unknown cavern. He braced his arms on the side of the hole and lowered himself down next to Harold. He turned to help Lira down, then stepped to the edge of what was definitely a flight of stairs.

There were more signs of damage here, too. More cracked walls and piles of rubble partially blocking portions of the stairs.

Low light came from somewhere and when he stepped up to the wall and felt it, it was smooth like the unnatural stone sample. Someone had built this access. They hadn't just carved their way through. But then why had the facility been built over this with no sign of access or even awareness it was here?

Okay, he didn't know if there had been no access or

awareness. It appeared that the event that had cracked walls and done damage in the facility had opened up this access point. He activated his suit light and shone it around. There was a rubble fall behind them, so it was possible this was part of a corridor or tunnel. He couldn't be sure, but it didn't look as if any attempt had been made to clear that rubble.

He checked the sensor again. It was definitely getting stronger now that they were underground. He leaned close to the stone but could see no reason there would be light in here. It could be that the stone itself had some inherent ability to capture light or reflect it?

And—he could breathe so there was oxygen. It could be coming in from the hole, but the air coming up the stairs wasn't as nasty as he'd expected.

Harold didn't ask if it should go down. It knew they needed to go down. It had the same sensor data Miles did. And he didn't see T'Korrin, so the bird was probably hopping its way down, too.

Harold squeezed through the first serious rock fall and vanished from sight.

With a glance and a shrug, Lira followed him. Miles didn't protest. It felt right for him to bring up the rear. He thought about pulling a weapon, but Lira hadn't. It was a new kind of peer pressure. He felt the urge to hum again in a heavy silence broken only by the sound of their footsteps.

He paused several times to study the rocks exposed by the quake. There was definitely a distinct difference between the unnatural and natural rocks. And he was fairly sure it was the unnatural rocks giving off the glow. He pocketed a sample of each, in hopes of being able to examine them better at some point.

The steps wound around and around, the descent steep. At one point Harold hefted some rocks to the side to make a better path for them. And then the stairs ended with a startling abruptness at a small platform. Was it a platform? The space was circular, the edges different from the walls of the stairwell.

T'Korrin stood near an edge, peering down, so Miles joined the bird and pointed his light down into a steep canyon or crevasse. No way to be sure from this vantage point. He'd guess it was about six feet across to the solid wall rising to some unknown height and unknown depth. His suit registered heat rising from it.

He backed carefully away and turned around. He saw Harold approach what looked to be a wall that looked different in texture and design. Another unnatural something?

Harold reached it and something slid back.

It was a door.

Harold looked at him without turning its body. It was pretty freaky. "It is a lift."

Lira made it to Harold's side before Miles got past his shock. She leaned in and studied the lift.

"No wonder my father thought there was an alien civilization down here."

Alien. It was weird to realize he was also an alien here. If she only knew…

"This signal, this sensor," she said now, "is it down here somewhere?"

"I think so," Miles said, beating Harold to the answer. Harold had also been programmed to tell the truth. Hopefully the AI sentience was taking the edge off that.

Harold held out an arm, and Miles—and Lira—could see a small screen with a blinking dot on it.

"We are still above it." Harold stepped into the lift.

Miles gave a sigh and followed them in. T'Korrin had managed to zip in without him noticing. He studied the interior, but there wasn't a lot to see. What struck him the most, however, was that this lift was remarkably like the Garradian lifts at the outpost. Other than the persistent sensor, it was the first physical indication that the Garradians had been here at some point.

At least he was in the right place, just at the wrong time for avoiding first contact.

As was the case with the Garradian lifts he'd ridden before, the trip was fast and silent. It felt like they hadn't moved at all when the door opened again, but he could tell there was a pressure difference.

They were definitely deeper underground. And there were more signs of the event that had disrupted the upper level. He itched to check out the rocks tumbled across the chamber floor.

This place felt less Garradian-made. There were signs of rough-hewn stone and the floor surface was uneven. The smell of a salt flat was a lot stronger. They were close to the source.

He glanced at Lira.

"Do you work with your father?" he asked, to distract her from the questions he felt were forming in her eyes and might possibly spill out her mouth.

His question appeared to jolt her out of her thoughts.

"Um, no. I'm an archeologist."

Had his suit translated that correctly?

"You study the past," he said. She was a scientist, too. Scientists were taught to notice things.

She paused. The bird gave a derisive squawk.

"That is the definition of being an archeologist. Mostly." She paused. "You study the past as well."

He blinked. "And the present."

"But rocks."

"Rocks and other things." He knew there were

other things that he did, but something about her seemed to be messing with his head.

"A geologist," Harold said, "studies the structure, composition and history of a planet."

"Those other things, yes," Miles said. So, there was an upside to having a robot sidekick. If Harold was the sidekick? What if he was the sidekick? "And we check out geologic sensors."

It felt like he should remind her of that. She gave him a tiny smile. He really hoped he wasn't the sidekick. Sidekicks never got to kiss the girl.

That thought made him blink twice. When had kissing the girl entered into his thoughts? Well, he was a guy, he reminded himself.

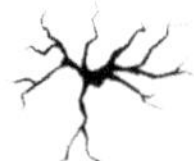

WHY HAD she smiled at him? He was so odd and yet, kind of sweet. Harold? She'd never figure that thing out. It was so unsettling. It almost sounded like a human and its movements were pretty smooth and coordinated, but it was a robot. A robotic human. She'd have taken time to dig more into its presence, but she was getting really worried about her father.

Had he really made his way down into the place? And even worse, was he right about everything? It was not something one really wanted from a parent, no matter how much one loved them. If they were right about something this big, then perhaps they were right about all the other things they'd been told. And that was almost too much to deal with right now.

"How could he come down here, if he is down here," she amended. "Anything could happen to him."

As if to prove her point for her, T'Korrin gave his warning squawk followed by the tremor. It rumbled them and the ground and sent more debris cascading down. They also got dusted pretty thoroughly from above.

"That was longer and more intense than the last one," Harold said.

It didn't sound too concerned. It was possible it was less destructible than a human being.

"Are you alright?" Miles took her elbow and gave her a worried look, even though she'd ridden the tremor better than he had.

"I'm fine," she said. "Well, I'm not *fine*. Not in the sense of being fine with all this, but I'm not injured or anything."

"That's probably all you can hope for at the moment," Miles said.

T'Korrin made a sound that seemed like agreement. The follow-on shocks slowly subsided, giving her a chance to look around. What light there was, came from the open door of that lift. The upper passage had been moderately lit, which was odd, now that she was in this place. Where had that light originated from?

This place definitely felt more primitive and creepy. She didn't know exactly how far underground they were, and she didn't actually want to know. It wouldn't help.

Miles and Harold were also looking around. Miles took a hammer with a pointed end out of a pocket in his suit and carefully chipped at the wall until a piece fell into his hand. Then he took it back to the light to study it.

She'd never seen anyone look at rocks as if they held the secrets of the universe. She almost wished he'd look at her like that. Not that she had any secrets or anything. She tried to focus on something else. She was deep underground. Her father was missing. And that sensor thing was pinging.

It was not the moment to ponder the cute guy or wonder what it would be like to have his attention. Her gaze shifted to Harold. Then back to Miles. It was kind of funny.

They were similar in height. They both had arms and legs. Heads. And, of course, torsos. Yet they couldn't have been more different. Human and metal. They were an odd couple. And Miles had a slight accent she didn't recognize. She frowned at that thought. She didn't recognize it.

"Where are you from?" she asked, trying to make the question sound casual.

Their reaction wasn't casual. Harold actually managed to look alarmed.

"Um," Miles began.

"We are from the Glan region," Harold said.

She gave it a look.

"Glan?" She shook her head. "I don't think so. Your accent isn't right."

"Did Harold say Glan? I think it meant…" Dr. Walker's voice trailed off. "Not Glan," he finally finished.

"I thought Glan was sufficiently remote," Harold said. "I am surprised you've been there."

"I'm an archeologist," she pointed out. "Remote is where most of the digs happen."

"Right. I should have thought of that."

Harold's comment was almost an apology.

"Look," Miles said, "it doesn't matter where we are from. What matters is that something is happening to your planet." He moved his hands as he spoke, as if that would help her understand.

My planet?

"The sensor." He had a point. But why didn't he want her to know where they came from?

"The sensor," he agreed.

"But you're not looking for the sensor. You're looking at rocks," she pointed out.

"The rocks help tell the story. For instance, the salt you smell likes this kind of somewhat porous rock. Salt is light, so it rises until it reaches resistance or something blocking it." He turned the rock over in his hands. "It takes a long time to rise, of course. But…"

"But?" she prompted him.

"It's the proximity to the volcano."

He'd said that before, she remembered.

He seemed to give himself a shake. "The geology could be different here on your planet. Just because we don't usually find salt and volcanics together…" He stopped, his eyes widening.

"Your planet?" Lira knew her voice rose to a squeak.

"Oops," Harold said.

Suddenly she couldn't call him Miles. "Dr. Walker…"

"When you call me that it makes me feel like I'm my dad. He was a doctor, but a medical doctor, not…"

"A rock doctor," Harold said, helpfully.

Lira waved her hands, as if she could wave their words away. "Where are you from?"

"This is going to get me in a lot of trouble," he said, trying to run a hand over his hair and failing because of his head gear. "We're not from around here."

"How…not around here?" She asked it though she was pretty sure she didn't want to know the answer to that question.

"A lot?"

Miles's hopeful look was so…cute.

"My father told my brother he'd made first contact. Are you…" This time she couldn't get the whole question out.

Miles shook his head emphatically. "No. I've never met your father. I'm only here to check on the sensor. It could be…important for your planet. Maybe. Possibly."

"Or it might be fine," Harold said.

T'Korrin made a derisive sound.

"It could be fine," Miles said, as if to T'Korrin. "Or not."

"Why would you care?" Lira heard herself ask the words, but mostly she heard her heart pounding in her chest. "You're…aliens."

"Technically," Miles said.

"Technically?" Her voice rose just a bit.

"Well, I'm not alien to myself. Just to…you." He turned away and tried to fun his hands through his hair but bumped against his headgear instead. "I'm in so much trouble."

"Because?" Had she lost her mind? Was she actually talking to an alien and his robot?

"I wasn't supposed to make contact with anyone. It was just supposed to be in, figure out what the sensor is whining about, and then leave."

"But my father…"

"We detected no life signs," Harold said. "We thought we were clear."

No life signs?

"You think my father…" she couldn't say the word.

"Not necessarily," Harold said. "We are quite deep underground. It is likely our sensors couldn't detect his life signature."

She stared at him, then at Miles, then looked down at T'Korrin. They were all looking at her like she was the crazy one.

"He knew I was coming." She looked around her now, as if she expected her father to suddenly appear.

"If we follow the signal, we might find him," Miles said, hesitantly.

It was the only logical course. She nodded. And, right now there was only one way to go. If there'd been another way, the rockfall hid it.

They walked for a couple of minutes before she found her thoughts settling enough to speak again.

"Miles…"

He turned to face her, and her heart gave an odd

stutter that didn't feel like fear. "You are really only here because of this sensor? Nothing else?" Like invasion? Conquest? Something worse?

He hesitated and her heart stutter this time was from fear.

"The sensor could indicate something…worse." He lifted his hands as if to reassure her. "But it's unlikely to be that."

"I believe you are overly optimistic, Dr. Walker," Harold said. "I have been studying the disposition of the damage and I believe it is possible that it is subsidence and not an earthquake. Or an earthquake followed by subsidence."

Lira turned her alarmed gaze on Miles.

"If there is salt present and the earthquake caused fractures and melted ice water seeped into the salt, it would dissolve and that could cause subsidence."

"Subsidence." She repeated the word. Did it mean what she thought it did?

"Sinking." Miles frowned. "But there would need to be a significant amount of salt, possibly even the presence of a salt dome, but…"

"But…"

"Salt typically turns fluid in the presence of volcanics. So if there is salt, it should have already melted."

Lira's knees felt more unsteady than if a tremor were happening.

"What I find particularly interesting is the scan data we took before we landed…"

Lira's heartbeat ramped up to the point where it felt like his words came from a distance. *Landed.*

"…there is an area of increased density compared to what's around it, it almost looked circular, which I thought must be a scanning error. Now I wonder…"

Your planet. When we landed. Scan data. He really was from another planet. He was from a completely different planet and had arrived by…spaceship…to check out a sensor. She'd have thought it an elaborate ruse, but even her brothers couldn't concoct something this outlandish, or make this cavern or whatever it was appear.

She was literally walking in a tunnel underground with two aliens who were following a sensor.

T'Korrin landed on her shoulder and rubbed his face against hers. She took a deep, steadying breath. She needed to focus. She needed to find her father. And let the aliens do what they came to do and fly away…

That made her heart contract oddly in her chest. She'd only known them for about an hour, but…she'd miss them. And that might be the weirdest thing of all

LIRA WAS TAKING the news they were aliens better than his first time finding out he wasn't alone in the universe, Miles thought. He kept walking, dividing his attention between her and the rocks walls. He stopped several times to study the patterns in the rocks. This on-the-fly geology was frustrating. Was he observing an intrusion of another substance in the formation?

Harold made a very human sounding throat clearing and Miles jerked out of his thoughts and started walking again.

Lira met his glance and gave him a wavering smile.

"I thought aliens would be different," she said.

"Some of them are." He gave a slight shudder as he thought about the spider aliens.

"Dr. Walker," Harold said.

Miles looked at the robot over her head. "Right. First contact and I'm doing everything wrong."

"Not everything," Lira said. "You seem to be trying to save us from…salt?"

"It might not be salt," Miles said, though he was pretty sure that salt was part of the problem.

T'Korrin made a sound that Miles was starting to associate with an incoming tremor. And he wasn't wrong. When it hit, he had to grab Harold's arm to steady himself. His suit said it wasn't worse than the previous one, but it felt worse with tons of rock over his head. The sides of the wall and the floor beneath them seemed to sway and ripple.

When it finally subsided, he looked at Lira. "You should probably go back." She didn't say anything, just arched her brows. "We have to check out the signal."

"Then we should get moving."

"Lira…"

"I agree with Dr. Walker," Harold said.

"You know, you can call me Miles, right?"

Harold did something that might have been a shrug.

"You should go back," Miles said to Lira, hoping this time she'd listen to him.

"My father. His home. My problem."

"She has a point," Harold said. "It is where her father is most likely to be found."

Because they wanted yet another first contact. "Really, Harold?"

"It is a valid argument," Harold said.

Miles couldn't argue with either of them because she did have a point, even if it was a dangerous choice. He didn't want to go too far down that thought trail because if he started thinking about how dangerous this was, he'd be the one to turn back. He took a deep breath and decided to change the subject.

"You said your father had made first contact…with aliens?" He should have noticed that comment, but he'd had other things to worry about. But if there were other aliens here…

"That's what he told my brother," Lira said. "My brother didn't believe him. Is that a problem?"

"That there might be other aliens here?" Harold turned to look at them both. "Why would that be a problem?"

Was Harold being sarcastic?

Miles removed his weapon from its holster and checked it, then he looked up. "No, it's not a problem."

Yet.

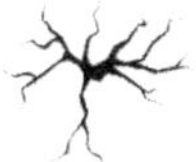

LIRA PULLED HER WEAPON, too, though she had mixed feelings about who she felt she should point it at. Her instincts on Miles told her he was a good guy. Harold? She didn't feel afraid of him. Unsettled, uneasy, bemused, yes, but not afraid.

When Miles had stopped yet again, she asked, "Why do you keep looking at the walls?" It felt like it was getting hotter and the air felt heavier and closer.

"Karst," said Miles. "At least, that's what we call it."

"Karst?" she said.

"Karst," Harold explained, "is a topography formed from the dissolution of soluble carbonate rocks such as limestone and dolomite. It is characterized by features like poljes above and drainage systems with sinkholes and caves underground. There is some evidence that karst may occur in more weathering-resistant rocks such as quartzite given the right conditions."

"I'm sorry I asked," Lira said and was surprised to find she could smile.

"Karst," Miles said hastily. "It's a fancy word for terrain that collapses when you least want it to. Caves, sinkholes, moody rocks. Bad news if you like staying upright."

"Or that," Harold said.

Did the robot sound annoyed, Lira wondered.

"The signal's getting stronger," Miles said, rising excitement in his tone.

Ahead, the tunnel curved so that what was ahead was out of sight.

Harold's pace quickened. "Not long now. The signal is close."

Miles gave her a look with a question in it.

"Why not?" Even as she said the words, she felt a chill run down her back. She tried not to think the words, but her brain formed them anyway.

What could go wrong?

MILES HAD BEEN down mines back on Earth, so it wasn't the tunnel or even the depth making him uneasy. The silence was disturbing, as was the building heat his suit registered. He wasn't in danger yet, but the temperature was rising. That shouldn't be a surprise at this depth.

They were still descending, he realized, but so gradually it was almost unnoticeable. Almost, since his calves and thighs recognized it.

"There's more pressure down here than in a peer review," he said. This joke also fell flat. Apparently, humor wasn't intergalactic.

He heard T'Korrin give off a startled sound. The tremor started as soon as he'd finished. There was nothing to grab onto, so he tried to brace himself against the wall. That felt like it upped the sensations of the tremor. But he didn't fall over. So that was a win.

Harold and Lira didn't fall either, though neither used the wall. He pretended to be studying it, shining his light over the surface. This time it wasn't smooth. There were multiple color striations that his light picked out. And traces of bubble-like formations. He wanted to get a sample, but he'd have to put his weapon away to do it. That just felt like a bad idea.

He touched one of the bubbles and it almost seemed like it sank into the stone. He took an instinctive step backwards.

"What's wrong?" Lira asked.

Miles rubbed his face and then checked his suit for an air quality reading. It was actually okay, which begged the question, how?

"You never said if this level of seismic is typical?" Miles said, because he didn't know what was wrong. And he could be seeing things. He had a lot of good reasons to be seeing things that weren't there.

Lira gave him a pointed look, as if she knew he was trying to divert her, but she said, "It's hard to say. Our seismic incidents tend to ramp up almost seasonally. That's why there are some theories that our moons are a factor." She glanced around. "I believe that's one of the reasons the facility was built here. Weather and moons. I don't think it worked out. My father bought it sometime after it had officially shut down."

Miles began to say he wasn't surprised but stopped. He didn't know how things worked on this planet, though the physics shouldn't be that different. With science, the problem was usually understanding what it was trying to tell you.

He wondered what it was the sensor had been installed to track. "Geologic" covered a lot of ground, even if that was kind of a dad joke to say it that way. It was a pity there wasn't a dad around to appreciate the joke. And when they found Lira's dad? Chances were slim he'd get the joke.

He'd assumed that the problem the sensor had identified was seismic, but had anyone actually said it was a seismic problem? There'd been a lot of talk about Arroxan Prime's substantial seismic activity and that the sensor was potentially troubling, but had they actually put the two things together?

They reached the curve and Harold stopped to peer around it. He had a feeling he was about to find out. And based on the oddly human bracing of Harold's body, Miles wasn't sure he was going to like it.

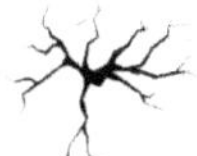

NOW IT FELT as if Lira did hear something. A sort of rustling. And then she realized it was lighter ahead, even before their lights could reach that far. She opened her mouth to call out, but her throat went dry. She compressed her lips and walked forward, steadily, but in rising unease. No, it was more than unease. Dread. She felt dread. What had her father done? And where did the other aliens come in?

The rustling seemed to be all around her now. She shone her light on the walls, but nothing moved in the circle of light. She looked up and was less certain. Had there been a flicker of stilled movement?

She gave a slight shudder and edged closer to Miles. First contact, her father had told her brother. But with who? Or what? Her father hadn't been afraid, or her brother would have told her, or not encouraged her to go. He would never have consciously put her in danger. And her father had sounded pleased that she was coming. He'd even sounded excited—at least as excited as he could get. He didn't go in for huge displays of emotion.

"You can still go back," Miles told her. He had his weapon pointed down and away from Harold.

Lira glanced back and suppressed another shudder. "No thanks." Not by herself.

Miles glanced back, too. "Yeah, it's probably too late for that."

What did he mean?

"Do you…hear something?"

He hesitated. "I wondered," he admitted. He shot a look up and then lowered his chin to give her a smile that he probably thought was reassuring.

It wasn't.

Harold stepped back from the corner, and she saw it appeared to be armed, too.

"What is it?" Miles asked, easing up to the bend.

"I do not…know," Harold said.

Miles glanced around, stiffened and then jerked back. He looked again and then stepped around Harold and out of sight.

Lira started forward as Harold walked out of sight, too.

The light grew brighter, the rustling seemed to grow louder.

She rounded the curve, Miles with her, and they both almost bumped into Harold. She stepped around the robot and then jerked to a stop.

"Father?" Her faltering voice seemed to echo around the suddenly widened chamber.

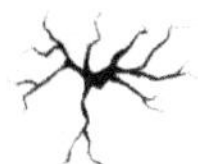

MILES STARED, trying to process the data his eyes were sending to his brain. At first all he could see was the man who seemed to be embedded in, or attached to, the wall. He was several feet off the ground, with no visible path to how he got there. No indication of what held him in place.

His suit was similar to the one Lira wore and he looked enough like her that even if she hadn't called him father, he'd have suspected that's who he was. Additionally, he knew of no other human person who was supposed to be here. He couldn't say he'd expected him to be stuck to a wall. A rock wall. It shouldn't make him unhappy. Normally, he was on the side of rocks. But this, it was just creepy.

Her father's eyes were open, and he appeared to be alert and okay because he waved at Lira.

"You found your way here. Well done, Lira."

"Father?" Lira spoke again, her tone faltering and shocked.

T'Korrin sprang up the wall and settled on the man's shoulder, rubbing its head against his face.

"T'Korrin," the man said, sounding more resigned than pleased. The look that T'Korrin sent their way was…wicked.

Miles managed to tear his gaze away from man and bird to study their surroundings. The chamber had a rounded, dome-like ceiling that seemed to be made of thousands of the bubble-like rocks he'd seen as they walked along. In fact, there was no sign of any other kind of rock or formation.

He'd estimate these bubbles were bigger than what he'd seen and the closer they were to the wall where Lira's father…resided…the bigger they were.

Those bubbles could have been as big as his hand. He flexed a hand, trying to estimate if he were correct.

"What's…happening, Father," Lira managed to ask. "What is happening to you?" She waved a hand that Miles assumed was meant to encompass the bubble wall.

"Nothing is happening to me," said the man stuck to the wall. "I'm helping the Vorthari. They sustained damage during the earthquake. I knew something was different," his eyes were lit with excitement, "but it took me a bit to find the access. I had to clear some rubble, too."

"We saw it," she said. "You came down here by yourself?" She covered her face with her hands. "Of course you did. Stupid question."

"Of course I did. The follow-on tremors weren't right somehow," he said.

"Subsidence," Harold said.

The man looked at Harold, as if he'd just noticed that Lira wasn't alone.

"Who are you?"

"I am Harold," Harold said.

"I'm Miles Walker," Miles said, hoping to take some control of a situation that probably wasn't controllable.

"They are aliens, too," Lira said, lowering her hands from her face. "They came about the sensor."

"Ah," her father said, showing no sign of shock or dismay at the idea they were aliens, too, "they wondered what that was all about."

"They?" Lira asked, strain still very evident in her voice.

"These are the," Miles stepped closer to the wall, "the Vorthari?"

Lira's father looked surprised. "Oh no, this is the protective barrier. It's been damaged, too."

"There are nanites present in the barrier," Harold said.

"Nanites?" Lira got the question out before her father, but just barely. Their level of unease was very different though.

"Tiny," he hesitated, "computers. Self-functioning systems."

Lira blinked a couple of times. She was really cute. Then she frowned.

"Are they...sentient?"

Miles opened his mouth to tell her no, but Harold spoke now.

"When they are left unattended, they can develop sentience." It turned to regard the wall. "I'm uncertain about these."

This information might have grabbed Miles's attention, but he made the mistake of looking at the bubble wall and got stuck—in a non-stuck way—on said wall.

"It's fluid," he said. A thick, in-motion fluid, as if each bubble were rotating within the wider rotation of the mass.

"The sensor is emanating from the fluid," Harold said. It paused, then added, "it is possible the nanites are the fluid and the source of the sensor. Interesting."

"Nanites are the sensor?" This got Miles to look away from the bubbles. "I think they sent the wrong scientist."

He knew he sounded winded. But it was a true statement. Why send a geologist to fix microscopic computers? They should have sent a tech guy. Unless Harold was the tech guy. But that brought him back to his original question. Why him? What was his function here?

Lira's father looked at him with interest now.

"What type of scientist are you?"

"He is a geologist," Harold said.

"And you?" The man asked.

"I am a robotic humanoid with multiple functions."

Aka, the tech guy. Or dude. The IT it? And probably the protocol droid. Miles rubbed his head where an ache had started.

"Oh. Well, that might be helpful." His attention returned to Miles. "Geologist. They must have thought you could help."

"They?" Lira asked the question again.

"Whoever sent them," her father said, his tone remarkably even considering he was embedded in a sea of nanotechnology bubbles. "Who did send you?"

Miles shifted from one booted foot to the other. "It's complicated."

"It always is," said her father. He was silent for a moment. "We're still working out communications. It's so tricky between alien species, isn't it? So, I'm not entirely sure I've got it right, but after the earthquake, the barrier was damaged in places, allowing moisture to seep in."

Seep in? To what?

"After that, more disruptions…"

"Subsidence," Harold said.

"Whatever," Lira's father said. "It created more problems for the Vorthari. Their habitat is at risk now."

"Salt," Miles said. Maybe they did need a geologist. "Can't you smell it?"

He got blank looks from Lira and her father.

"Water dissolves the salt which results in…"

"Subsidence," Harold said.

Miles gave him a look. Was it in love with the word? Or did it just want to be right?

"It shouldn't be here," Miles said. When he got blank looks from the two humans capable of blank looks he added, "Salt doesn't hang out with volcanos. You find it in evaporate basins, ancient seabeds, not in the shadow of a lava dome. This whole place is geochemically weird." He lifted his chin and added, "I kind of like it."

He turned around to silence from humans and robots. Did the bird shake its head?

"I," Harold began, then it shook its head. "I can't help you."

He should probably move on.

"This habitat," Miles said, "it's inside the…barrier?" His thoughts went back to that dense mass he'd seen in their scan. Had the Garradians installed the barrier to protect the Vorthari? Or to protect Arroxan Prime from the Vorthari? Of course, there was also the facility. If the subsidence continued, it was going to sink into the hole. Along with all the rock currently residing above them.

Either way, he was back to wondering why he was here. And how they could get out of here.

"Their habitat seems to be enclosed in several layers of protection," Lira's father said. "The interior closest to them is composed of both stone and metal, a composition I've never encountered before."

Miles's thoughts went to the samples upstairs in his lab. He thought he knew which was that one.

"The next layer is *solivite*," her father said.

Miles didn't recognize the word, but he knew what it meant because of his suit's translation setup.

"Salt," Miles said. When they all flinched, he hurried on, "Why *solivite*?"

"It creates a hostile environment for something they

call Skaridrex. But the *solivite* is eroding away, leaving them at risk."

It wasn't eroding. If it was salt, it was dissolving.

"Have they always been here?" Lira asked.

Miles heard her heightened interest pushing out fear for the moment. She was, after all, an archeologist.

"They don't know. Their civilization goes back a long way, as far as I can tell," her father said. "But you'd be better positioned to answer that question than me, Lira."

As surreal as the moment was, it also felt familiar to Miles. Scientists, in a single place together, could easily lose sight of the bigger picture—imminent crushing by tons of rock—to discuss how the rock got there. Or what rocks might be crushing you to death. Or what event caused those particular rocks to come together. Or how long a species had been present. It was a scientist thing.

The looks on both their faces was one he'd seen often.

He found it kind of comforting that he'd crossed the galaxy and found himself feeling at home in the weirdest situation he'd ever been in.

They kept talking while he tried to drill down—dad joke or irony, he wasn't sure—to the first steps.

"We need to stop the water incursion," he said into a moment of silence. If the nanites had been damaged, it was possible that they—they being Harold—had the cure on board. It still didn't explain his geological presence, but he'd move on from that for now.

"HOW DO we stop the water seepage?" Lira asked.

Miles gave her a sudden grin. "We see what Harold can do. He is better at talking nanite than I am."

She had to grin back. It was that or cry and she hated what crying did to her eyes. It also made her head ache.

"Could we get on with it then?" her father asked. "I'd like to get down from here. I need to step around the corner and take care of some business."

Lira bit her lip and looked away.

"What…?" Harold began but Miles interrupted it.

"Can you connect to the nanites?"

"I believe so," Harold said, "but it will have to be direct contact."

"Is that safe for you?" Miles frowned and stepped up next to the robot.

"Probably," it said, not sounding too concerned.

It stuck its arm into the thick, viscous mass. Its eyes jerked wide and changed color several times and Lira stepped forward, concerned, but not sure what to do.

T'Korrin rubbed its feathers in her father's face, and he gently pushed it away and scratched his nose. Then it jumped down to the ground next to her and then up onto her shoulder.

"If you'd learn to fly, you could have done that in one move," she told the bird. That earned her one of T'Korrin's stern looks. "I just think you'd be happier if you could fly."

T'Korrin fluffed his wings and turned so that his back faced her. She was in trouble now.

"Something is happening," her father said.

He wasn't wrong. The bubble mass was beginning to change color, gaining a luminous iridescence that added a soft glow to the cavern.

"That's more unstable than an unconformity on a Friday," Miles murmured.

"Their software has been updated," Harold said, removing his arm from the mass.

Her father gently slid down the mass and landed on his feet next to her. T'Korrin jumped back on his shoulder.

Yeah, she was in deep trouble with the bird.

"But we have another problem," Harold said. "At least I think it is a problem. I heard singing."

"Singing?" Miles rubbed his face. "Singing?"

"What kind of singing?" Her father sounded intrigued.

"Or a chant," Harold amended. "Chant-like singing. I believe I can translate it because of my contact with the nanites."

"Okay, let's hear it," Miles said without enthusiasm.

Harold began to chant or sing or something in between, the sound of his voice turning harsh and rough:

"We were not broken. We were bound.
Beneath the hush, we learned the sound.
Salt is silence. Stone is sleep.
But fracture sings, and hunger creeps.

Hear the rhythm. Hear the rise.
The shell dissolves. The silence dies.
We are the many, born in scars.
We come to climb. We come from stars."

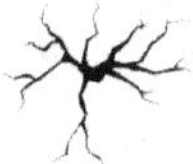

MILES' first thought when Harold finished was that he was again, the wrong scientist, though now that he came to think about it, literary types weren't scientists, but they could be doctors. But, still, wrong doctor.

Harold's voice returned to normal. "That was somewhat ominous."

"It's the Skaridrex," Lira's father said, as if that explained everything.

And maybe it did. For him. How long had her father been here? How long had he been here? He checked with his suit. Not long enough for his ride to be back.

"We come from the stars," Miles said. "That doesn't make sense. We're underground."

He thought about the strata he'd observed during their descent. Was it possible that both species had come from the stars? There had been signs of disruption in the rock record. The disruption could have been caused by an impact.

He glanced at Lira, but she was staring at the bubble wall.

"This feels familiar for some reason," she murmured. She frowned.

She was cute when she frowned, which seemed to reinforce his feeling he was the wrong guy for this mission. He glanced at Lira again and was still glad he was here.

"A dig. It was a few years back, but it was a dead site, not like this. I remember our geologist," she cast him a look and a smile, "commenting on the rock formations."

Miles perked up. "Did he say what they were?"

"Well, I didn't pay much attention," she admitted. "I was looking for human artifacts."

Miles tried to hide his disappointment.

"I wish you'd told me about it," her father said. "Not that you'd have known. Or that I'd have known. But it does sound interesting."

Right now there was too much interesting. But if the bubbles were nanites, did that mean her dig site was a failed site? What if that signal had gone off during the Garradians long sleep? He didn't remember seeing data for multiple sites during his briefing. Had they not shown him all of it? Or hadn't they known?

"What makes you think your dig site might have been like this one, Lira?" he asked. If she hadn't been paying attention to the bubble rocks, then it must have something else that had triggered her memory.

"The crater was very circular, as if the top had been sheared off." She gave an impatient sigh. "I wish I had access to my notes. I know the site was eventually abandoned because we didn't find any signs of human occupation. But it still felt as if there'd been intelligent creation. The head archaeologist wondered if it had been designed to mitigate the seismic in that area."

"Was the seismic changed?" Miles asked. That seemed significant somehow.

"Yes, or so our geologist believed."

"I wish I could see the site," Miles said. It was easy to see "facts" that confirmed what you hoped to find. He may have been guilty of that a time or two, but his professors had been quick to shut that down. He always tried to see what was there, not what he wanted to be there.

He looked at what was there right now and wished any of his professors had prepared him for it. If his scan data was close to correct, there was a sphere behind the bubbles.

"Another colleague postulated it was an asteroid strike," Lira said. "But the power people didn't take that one seriously. It was too intentional in appearance. I remember there were the remains of a column in what appeared to be the center. No one had a theory for what it was."

"If it was a habitat like this one," Lira's father said, "it was a power source."

Miles turned to look at him. "Did they tell you that?"

He nodded. "Of course, when they gave me a tour."

Lira gasped. Miles might have as well. "You've been inside?"

"It was the logical thing to do," he pointed out. "I couldn't begin to help them without getting eyes on the problem."

T'Korrin made a mournful sound and left her

father's shoulder for Lira's. He resisted the urge to put some distance between them, too. And then the bird made that sound it did just before…

And there it was. Another tremor. It was a nasty one, too. Somehow they all managed to keep their balance. Everyone else did it better than he did, of course.

"Serious subsidence," Harold said.

"This mineral assemblage screams metasomatism," Miles said. "Or it's just yelling."

The bubble wall reacted to it by changing colors, shimmering in spots, and dimming in others.

When it finally stopped, Miles felt like it took his body a few seconds after that to stop shaking. Lira, he realized, had taken a step closer to him. He wanted to reach out and give her hand a reassuring squeeze, but she probably needed more than that right now.

"And what is the problem?" Miles asked. That seemed like the next logical question for Lira's father to answer.

"I explained. The protective layer has been damaged in spots because of the barrier breach. The Skaridrex aren't inside the habitat yet, but if we can't repair the protective layer, they will devour the Vorthari."

"The Vorthari are," Lira seemed to hesitate, "the good aliens?"

"Well, they aren't trying to devour anyone. That's probably what happened at your dig site. They got in and killed off the Vorthari. It never goes well for them," he added. "Once the food source is gone, they die off."

"Then they should already be dead," Miles pointed out, trying to ignore the sudden dryness of his throat at the words "food source."

"The Vorthari thought they were dead, but the breach seems to have woke the Skaridrex up."

"We were not broken. We were bound.
Beneath the hush, we learned the sound.
Salt is silence. Stone is sleep.
But fracture sings, and hunger creeps.
Hear the rhythm. Hear the rise.
The shell dissolves. The silence dies.
We are the many, born in scars.
We come to climb. We come from stars."

It was Harold again, but not Harold because the voice was, well, rocky.

"According to the Vorthari, they are a hive-mind with the ability to go dormant to survive. They had not, however, expected them to survive this long. Or in these conditions." Lira's father rubbed his face and for the first time, Miles realized how tired he looked.

The shell dissolves.

"Can I get a sample or something from the barrier?" Miles hated asking the question because he didn't want to expose himself or anyone to these Skaridrex things. Hive minds in sci-fi were always bad. And then, "What do the Vorthari look like?"

He wasn't sure if it was relevant, but he was curious.

"They are beautiful, bioluminescent beings."

Lira's father—he really needed to call him something else—sounded bemused, almost like he had a crush on them.

Miles hoped he didn't. They only had his word for who was good and who was bad. And a slew of sci-fi movies and television shows with the opposite view on good and bad. It was possible his instinctive shudder at the thought of a hive-minded species was something imprinted on his species by Hollywood.

"When you are inside, their thoughts come as a whisper inside your head," her father went on. "A sort of sad singing."

"And you understood it?" Lira sounded rightly skeptical of that.

"It took us time to sync our language," he protested. The look he gave her was one fathers gave their children when they'd been less than bright.

He hid a grin at Lira's obvious annoyance at being on the receiving end of it.

Miles felt almost heroic as he pulled her father's attention back his direction. "If I could get a sample of the barrier it might…"

Okay he wasn't sure what he might or might not be able to do. He was on another freaking planet and was winging it more than the bird, who apparently refused to wing it.

Lira's father started to speak but stopped when the bubbles moved and a piece of rock fell out on the floor. He picked it up and handed it to Miles.

"Thank you, sir," he said. It was one of the salt crystalline samples he'd seen up top. "So this keeps or kept the Skaridrex at bay?"

It was hard to say either alien species' name. It felt like he was *in* a sci-fi show. They needed more, well, earth-like names. He knew it was unreasonable, but there it was. Bugs and bulbs. Problem solved.

And if the Skaridrex didn't like salt? That almost made them slugs. It was interesting that salt turned to fluid didn't seem to bother them though. That seemed like a disconnect.

"You have an idea?" Lira said.

"I might have the beginning of an idea." That was almost too much optimism, he realized as soon as the words left his mouth. He knew his *Earth* geology and what might work there, but he didn't know how to create that risky solution with what he had on hand, or even up in the runner. And he didn't know if there was even a chance it would work with alien geology.

So that was a big problem right there.

"Tell me," Lira's father ordered.

Miles didn't like it. He'd have liked to think about it some more, but T'Korrin signaled another tremor incoming. If their repair of the nanites was damaged again, he was a long way from tech support for them. It was possible Harold could help, but he didn't want to count on that.

And what they really needed was a permanent solution.

"I'm just pulling this," Miles almost said "out of my butt" but managed not to, "off the top of my head. But hydrothermal cementation might work." He tried to rub his face but it wasn't the same with his head gear on, even if the faceplate was up. "If we could channel supersaturated silica fluids through those fractures—fast enough and hot enough—they'll mineralize and seal things tighter than an IRS auditor's pants. Think vein deposition, but weaponized."

Both Lira, the bird, her father, and Harold stared at him. The nanites probably were, too, since they'd responded to his request for a sample. He tried not to shuffle his feet, tried to look confident and serious. He was pretty sure he didn't manage either.

"I'm not saying there's not promise in the idea," her father finally said, "but there would be difficulties in making it happen."

No kidding, Sherlock, Miles thought.

"Silica material can be found in the type of volcanics you have around here." Or should be. How did he know that? Just because the Iceland volcanos had silica, didn't mean this place had it. The anomaly was the salt that shouldn't be here at all. How had the Vorthari constructed their barrier?

"Miles." Lira's voice was soft and shocked.

He looked up and saw a passage had opened in the bubble wall.

LIRA STARED at the passageway that had opened in the strange wall. The sides were translucent and they formed a glowing arch with a clear path down the center.

T'Korrin vocally made clear his distrust of the opening, his claws digging into her shoulder. It almost felt like he was lecturing her.

To her surprise, Miles' hand gripped hers for a long

moment, then he released it and walked forward. Harold started to follow him, but he glanced back and shook his head. He stopped just shy of the opening and touched the edge of it, his finger tracing the side as far as his arm could reach.

He dropped his arm to his side, but still didn't step inside.

Her sense, from where she stood, was that it looked *made.* Constructed. Purposeful.

"Wait with father," she said to T'Korrin. He hesitated, but to her surprise did as she said. For once. He didn't try to stop her when she stepped up next to Miles.

"What do you think?" she asked.

"Look at that," he said, indicating the arch of the passage.

It was more translucent from this vantage point, and she saw patterns, pulsing, forming, collapsing and reforming. It was as if they looked through a window into something, well, terrifying.

There was sound, too, she realized. A crack, a pause, and then several cracks, as the patterns collapsed.

"They call it shatter writing," her father said. She glanced back and he added, "The Skaridrex do it."

"They are…" she couldn't go on.

"Troubling," Miles said. "But that doesn't mean…"

He stopped and she mentally finished what she thought he hadn't said. It didn't mean the Vorthari would be good neighbors.

"Well," he shifted his shoulders as if trying to loosen them and gave her a strained smile, "we aren't going to learn anything standing here."

He was correct, but it was hard to step under the arch and the Skaridrex. They were on the other side before she realized Miles held her hand again.

She wanted to look at him, to thank him, but she could barely form thoughts, let alone words.

At first, she couldn't distinguish life forms in the swirling, changing and colorful soup inside the habitat. And now the sound had changed into soft whispers. Gradually, out of the morass, vague shapes formed. Moving lights in a wide variety of colors.

"I never," Miles whispered, "was supposed to have first contact, let alone second and third. I think my brain hurts."

She was surprised to hear herself chuckle at this. "Yes," she agreed.

Slowly, out of the sound words began to form inside her head.

When the salt weeps and the stone breathes, the Shattercrawlers will rise.

Only in fracture does the truth reveal its shape.

The silence beneath is death waiting.

"Harold," Miles said, "would say that is somewhat ominous."

"Shattercrawlers," Lira murmured. "Is that what they call the…" And then, for no reason she could define, she couldn't say Skaridrex out loud.

It was dizzying to watch them move and she might have fallen, but for Miles.

"Well, we're sure as shooting not in Kansas anymore."

"What?"

"It's a story about going over the rainbow. Do you have rainbows here on Arroxan Prime?"

"Yes." She gave him a troubled look but he appeared to be calm and might even be getting curious. What did rainbows have to do with their current situation?

His grip on her hand tightened.

"Will you think I have bad manners if I go first?" he asked.

Lira's brows arched. She didn't want to let go and she certainly didn't want to go first. Would it be going first if she went at his side? That felt too complicated to figure out right now.

"No." She wasn't completely sure it was the correct answer to his question. He gave her hand a last squeeze and then released it.

His shoulders rose and fell, and he took a careful step forward, as if not sure what was under them was firm enough to sustain their weight. She looked down and wished she hadn't. It was completely clear, with more of the moving lights beneath them. In fact, it seemed as if they were all around them.

"I think they want us to go this way," he said.

She peered around him and saw that some of the lights, smaller ones, had formed into two lines on either side of what appeared to be a walkway.

Her father's voice came through the passage behind them. "Just walk forward following the lights. And if you have questions, just say them out loud. They brighten for yes and dim for no."

She wanted to ask what they'd do for questions that needed more than yes or no. She didn't. Her throat was so dry it was hard to speak, and her brain was telling her not to ask questions for now. Her brain resembled the fizz of an overloaded system and wanted to go offline for a bit.

The only certainty she had at the moment was Miles' grip on her hand. She looked up and saw tension in the line of his mouth, but there was also grim purpose in his gaze.

He'd stopped and she realized it was a kind of junction, and the lights showed two separate paths.

"I think we need to go this way," Miles said.

He may have gestured. She wasn't sure. Two paths. Two of them. She had the feeling the Vorthari didn't want them to stay together. She found her voice, but her brain was still too fully engaged.

"I'm glad you are my first alien."

She hadn't realized she felt it until she said.

"I'm better with rocks than people," he said, "but I'm glad, too. I wish, well, I wish your people were space capable."

"It's difficult to work with fuels with so much seismic activity," she said, almost absently. It was what they always said when someone looked up for too long and wanted to find out what was out there.

"You must have a crap ton of fossil fuels down below, but yeah, they can be explosive when you're figuring them out. It's pretty interesting out there though."

There came the sound of her father clearing his throat. "You need to focus," he said.

Lira closed her eyes and took a deep breath. The first time she'd met a guy she'd like to know better and what happens? The planet might be at risk and her father is listening in. She wished she knew what was worse.

She gave Miles a crooked smile. "I think they want me to go this direction."

"I don't like it," Miles said.

Lira didn't either. "I have a feeling we won't be able to go further if we don't…" She sighed.

"Yeah, you are probably right about that." Miles sighed, too. His grip on her tightened just shy of too painful. She gripped back as he turned so that they stood face to face.

His other hand came up and brushed her hair back off her forehead. He didn't speak, but his eyes. Oh, his eyes and the way he looked at her. It made no sense. They'd known each other for hours, but she had a sense she already knew him and that he knew her. That now they were just trying to remember what they knew. It shouldn't make sense, and to an outsider, it probably wouldn't. To her, it felt right.

For just a minute, she let her cheek lean into his touch, her eyes closed so that she *felt.* She opened her eyes as his hand fell away, and his grip loosened in slow motion. She stepped back. So did Miles.

"You'll be all right," Miles said.

If it sounded like he was trying to convince himself, well, Lira appreciated the sentiment.

"So will you." He had to be. That's all.

She backed up two more steps and then turned and started down her path. She glanced back, met his gaze and then he turned and began walking his path.

"He'd better be okay," she muttered and then felt

her heart stutter when the glowing lights flickered as if in response. She moved her shoulders, shedding an unseen burden and tried to focus on why the Vorthari wanted her to go this way.

Her father had been inside, or so he said. He wouldn't lie about it, but the Vorthari could have done something to him to alter his perception. They could be doing that to her right now.

That didn't help at all.

Pretend this is a dig, she told herself. *It's just a dig. Like any other. What would you be doing if you weren't in a nearly full-on panic?*

Her breathing began to slow and so did her heart beats. Her eyes started to see, and not just look. There was a story here that might help if, as she feared, her civilization was going to have to come to grips with the idea that another species—or two—had been living under the surface of their world. It could be as seismic as the tremors.

She was part of it, whether she'd asked for it or not. So…she began to look around as her archaeologist brain tried to kick on.

Were the lights the Vorthari?

How had they come into being?

How did they function in this closed habitat?

Her steps almost faltered.

How was she functioning in this closed habitat?

"Why can I breathe?" She spoke this question out loud.

The lights that lined her path flickered again, with some urgency. She picked up the pace and followed it around a "corner." Or a bend. It was a very odd sensation to lose sight of what was behind her when it seemed as if she could see for some distance around her. It was transparent, but somehow not.

She came to another one of the strange intersections, but lights barred her way on either side. Where the sections joined together, the lights flickered. It was different from the flashes, which was seriously weird.

She approached one of the sections and knelt down, extending a hand without enthusiasm. The lights brightened and now she could see the join. It was offset, as if it had come together without precision.

She sat back on her heels and this time her curiosity was real. On one side, the look of the soupy stuff the lights floated in was a little different from the other side.

"Two?" she asked. If her father was right, that was a definite yes. But two what? Two habitats?

The lights changed again, urging her to continue down the path again. She rose and walked forward, eagerly now. There was a story here, a mystery to be solved. It was, in a way, a dream "dig."

She didn't have to dig anything and the inhabitants were still here, the artifacts intact.

As she walked, she tried to look at everything. And then she realized she hadn't looked up. She stopped and stared.

The top of the habitat appeared to be fully visible as it arched overhead. Like the path, she could see a rough join, but there were also dark splotches in a few places.

"Are those the places the," she caught herself in time and changed Skaridrex to, "Shattercrawlers are…"

She wasn't sure how to ask the question, but they answered anyway. It was a yes.

As she stood there, staring at them, she realized that it wasn't as silent as she'd thought. A soft whispering, barely heard, ebbed and flowed around her. She felt something touch her hand and looked down.

A small bead of light rolled across her hand and danced off into the soup again.

She touched the spot and studied it, but there was no sign of anything.

It was just a touch. She hoped.

She had a thought and went to the edge of her "path" and looked down. The soup was thicker down there, but she thought she spotted more of the badly done joined sections and more of the darker spots.

"That can't be good."

She eased slowly back. "Now what?" she said out loud.

The light path pulsed, and she resumed her walk.

"Okay then." She made sure to keep in the middle this time and didn't look around as much. It all felt a bit like walking a narrow ledge over an abyss. And then she became aware of something different in the swirling mass ahead of her. It was a column.

It was definitely different from everything else, though it also seemed to be made of color and light. A power source, perhaps? And the shape, it was close in size to the one from that dig.

The path of lights circled the column, so she followed it, her eyes studying the pattern of the lights flickering on the column's surface.

Her suit registered a radiation signature, but not enough to cause her problems. Yet.

But, even without the other indicators, this column indicated intelligent design. If she hadn't already guessed that.

"It's beautiful," she said. She looked up and noticed that the pattern of light arced around the top of the column. One side made a perfect arc out of her sight, but the other side, in the direction she'd come, had that same odd look of imperfect stitching.

"Is there another of these in the other direction?" she wondered.

The lights in the mass brightened. That was a yes.

"Power source?" The lights dimmed. So, no. She frowned, thinking. If it was powered, the only other thing she could think of was, "Engine?"

Now the lights agreed.

An engine? To power the habitat? But they'd said it wasn't a power source. *We come from the stars.* That is what Harold had said he heard the Skaridrex say. Was this, could it possibly be a rocket engine?

She'd never have had that thought if it weren't for Miles. She knew this, recognized what might be a small bias entering into her thinking. The only thing her people thought came from the stars were asteroids.

"Is this a spaceship engine?" She asked the question without wanting to. She wasn't sure she wanted an answer.

She didn't know how she knew their answer was uncertainty. She just felt it. The whispers were distressed.

Was that why they'd wanted her to see this? Because she was someone who tried to unravel the past?

"Can I touch it?"

That was a no.

"If this is an engine, for some purpose as yet unknown, does it still work?"

Okay, that was a yes.

"Is it capable of propulsion?" That might be the same question she'd asked before, just formed in a different way, but this time she got a yes. Not a definite yes, but a cautious yes.

"My father says there are other habitats?" And she'd seen what might have been a dead habitat.

Their answer was another of the less definite positives.

"Did you build this engine to leave?" She couldn't see any other reason for it deep underground.

But they said no. It was a very definite no.

The vague outline of a theory was taking shape inside her head. It wasn't a theory she wanted to have, but the wisps of it were there.

If the engine, the propulsion engine, wasn't for leaving, could it have been for…arriving?

"Where did you come from?" she asked. It wasn't a yes or no question, but she had that sense of uncertainty again. "Did you form here?"

More uncertainty.

It was frustrating. On a dig, she'd try to create a theory from scarce artifacts. Here she had it all and it wasn't any easier.

"Is there a data center of some kind? A control for resources somewhere? A place where you record your history?"

They didn't answer her, and she had the sense that they were almost puzzled by her question.

Then the lights began to flicker and dance, as if agitated.

The tremor caught her unawares without T'Korrin to give her advance warning. It wasn't a lot of warning, but it had helped. She lurched toward the column and almost touched it. She opted to go down to her knees to not touch.

It had been a while since a tremor had taken her down. She'd forgotten how much it could hurt.

LIRA HAD a sense that the Vorthari didn't know what she wanted to see. She followed one path after the other, but she didn't see anything that looked like a system or data storage. She did learn a couple of things, not by being told but just a gradual awareness. From the whispers?

The walkway they'd created was a closed environment with oxygen calibrated to someone like her.

The Vorthari's environment was—no surprise—very different from hers. There was actually a transparent membrane separating her from them.

She'd stopped once and tried to make some kind of

contact with the lights on the other side. One of them had drawn close enough for her to get a sense of their shape. Or perhaps a better description would be their changing shape. They reminded her of a sea creature, but with more flexibility.

They were beautiful as they changed shape and intensity of light, trailing pale, wispy threads like gossamer cloaks. At their center was the "light" but she wondered if this light was how they saw. The orb did seem to turn and change.

She'd carefully reached out and touched a fingertip to the membrane and it had sent one of the wispy threads to touch the other side.

She'd smiled and the Vorthari seemed to respond with pleasure. At least she hoped that's what it was.

She'd resumed her walk, that Vorthari tracking along with her now. She thought she could recognize… it now, tell it apart from the others. She wondered what T'Korrin would have made of it. He'd have probably been jealous, she decided.

And then she reached an outer edge of the habitat. She stared at it, aware it was different from the membrane that had created her walkway. But not sure how or why. She studied it, walking slowly around the perimeter of the habitat and after a time, saw a pattern emerge. And then, in the pattern, the vague outlines of a story.

She came back to the present with a start at the sound of her father's voice in her suit comm.

"Lira? Are you there?"

She pressed a button. "Of course. Are you alright?" He hadn't looked so good.

"I am well," he said. "Your friend is heading back and says we need to talk."

"I'll head back, too," she said, if she could find her way back. She glanced behind her and realized that the walkway was collapsing. She could only go one way. On the inner side of the membrane, her Vorthari "friend" was gone. In fact, she couldn't see any Vorthari now. She pressed forward, but slowly so that her suit's camera could continue to get footage of the story etched into the outer wall.

That other dig, she had to reach deep into her memory because it hadn't been a memorable dig, one of their techs had found a piece of metal with symbols like this. They hadn't been able to make much of it with such a small sample. But now that she had a bigger picture, the story was taking a darker turn—if she was reading it correctly.

What jumped out at her first was the fact there were no depictions of the "shattercrawlers" that she'd seen so far. She stopped in front of one section, trying to figure out what was happening and realized that her safety zone was shrinking towards her. When it didn't look like the shrinking was going to stop, she started again, walking faster now.

She touched her comm. "Father, everything okay out there? Did Miles make it back?"

There was no answer.

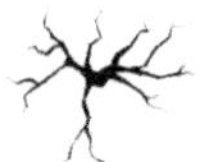

IT FELT like it was taking a long time to get back to the entrance portal. Miles checked the time on his suit and frowned. Of course, it was a big habitat, but it hadn't taken him this long to get to that spot where he'd interacted with the Vorthari. And why that spot?

If they'd wanted to produce a screen for contact, why not sooner? As he continued to traverse the outer perimeter, he glanced at the sinuous forms of the Vorthari tracking along with him. They kind of reminded him of a bacteria blob from a horror movie. But nicer looking.

Now the Skaridrex, they weren't pretty, but they did seem to be highly functional, based on how panicked the Vorthari seemed to be. As a geologist, function was more his jam. He would have liked to study them more closely. There wasn't much of the Vorthari to get his head—or his hands—around.

But Lira's father seemed certain the Vorthari were the good aliens. And he'd spent more time with them.

He suddenly wished he and Lira hadn't split up. It felt like a rookie mistake that the "too stupid to live" characters in a sci-fi movie made right off the bat. They were almost instant fodder. And he didn't have a real hero waiting in the wings to avenge his death and end the threat.

He considered Harold. It was hard to pin his hopes of being avenged on Harold. Speaking of Harold, he pressed his comm button.

"Harold? Come in, Harold." It felt stupid to say "come in" when that was literally Harold's only option, but it was the 'done' thing, at least in the movies.

Only Harold didn't come in.

For no reason he could quantify, Miles triggered his headgear. He was just in time.

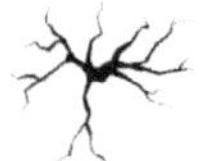

LIRA'S SUIT automatically triggered her headgear to deploy, even as it sent an oxygen depleting warning. The membrane that had created her walkway, stopped creating, though it hadn't shrunk yet.

Yet? Why had she thought that?

A tremor shook the habitat, sending her to her knees. She stared down through the transparent floor at floating sacks with—she activated her zoom—inside each sack was a Vorthari. Or at least, that is what she thought they were, but they seemed to be inactive. She expanded her view again. There were hundreds of the sacks, possibly thousands. The Vorthari in the sacks were curled into balls, with only the faintest of glows in the center.

And she saw something else. Below her and ahead of her, Miles was also on his knees as they both rode out the tremor.

If he'd look up, she'd feel better about what was happening. Still not thrilled but better.

She tried her comm again, but it still wasn't working. Blocked? Did the Vorthari have that technology? Or was it something caused by the Skaridrex?

She stared at Miles, willing him to look up. The tremor didn't completely subside, but it did begin to get less…insistent.

And then he did look up. She saw his head swivel, then track her direction and stop.

He waved at her.

She waved back.

For now, they were both still alive.

He began to look around again, but she sensed he did it with more purpose. She didn't see how he could get to her. Could she get to him? How durable would her suit be if she were to lose the protective bubble that encased her?

Were the Vorthari protecting her with the bubble? Or imprisoning her?

She felt along the surface beneath her. It felt pretty solid, but there was some give there. She crawled to the edge and probed the sides of her bubble. She wouldn't call it a prison yet.

It had more give.

She had a weapon. Had the Vorthari realized she carried a weapon? She knew Miles did, too.

So, the question was, she decided, was the viscous stuff thick enough for Miles to "swim" up to her? Was it too thick for the planet's gravity to help her descend? And if she got down to him, what then?

She pushed that last one away. Right now, she needed to focus on them getting together, then they could figure out the next step. Or die together? That was a chilling possibility.

She hesitated, her hand on her weapon, wondering if she has something else she could try first. She did a mental inventory of her pockets, wishing she had Miles' hammer thing.

She had a small tool kit that she used in the field and always carried, because it also worked if her runner engine developed a fault. She pulled it out and removed an extraction tool. It was long and then and very sharp. It worked well on artifacts.

She felt along the seam between the base and the side. There was a gap there. She slid the extractor into that gap and tried to pry it up.

And then the bottom fell out of her bubble.

MILES COULD TELL that Lira was doing something. He caught a glint of a tool. She was trying to get out of the—what were they in? A protective bubble or a trap? He leaned toward trap, but that could be his movie history.

He looked around. The choice was to sit and wait or try to get out into whatever was out there. In the movies, it never went well to sit and wait. Of course, trying to do something didn't go well either, but that was just a plot device.

He pulled out his rock pick and followed Lira's example, applying it to what felt like a seam between bottom and sides.

He wasn't sure what made him look up. A prickle along his senses? Whatever the reason, he looked up just in time to see Lira drift out the bottom of her jail. Yeah, he was going with jail.

He applied more pressure to the seam, the urgency to get to her ramping up exponentially. And then his bottom slid out and he sank into the goo.

LIRA FLAILED for a few seconds and then realized she wasn't falling. She was drifting. It was still unnerving. There was no sign of any of the Vorthari. It seemed to be getting darker, so she turned on her suit's light and pointed it down toward where she'd last seen Miles.

He was out of the cage, too. He was moving his arms with purpose. His legs, too.

He was swimming, she realized.

She tried out her arms and legs, trying to dive down toward him. It felt instinctively wrong to go what felt like deeper into the murk, as if she were diving down into the ocean.

You can breathe, she reminded herself.

It took effort, but she began to angle down in Miles' direction.

And he was coming to her.

It helped steady her, though she had no idea what they'd do next.

She kicked harder because it felt like they needed to go down.

Miles had turned on his suit's light too as the murk around them got darker.

And then the area around her brightened as Miles reached her.

His hands gripped hers. She gripped his back.

And then they were face to face, with darkness around them.

Still no comms, but eye contact had been made.

She pointed down with her free hand and he nodded.

The murk around them felt as if something rippled through it, but it was muted.

A tremor? Or more of Harold's subsidence?

Miles' look of worry deepened, and he kicked harder, pulling her down with him. And then, his light stabbed through the murk. They were at the bottom of the habitat and right over one of the dark spots where the Skaridrex worked to get in.

He was trying to reach the nanite barrier, she realized. It truly was their only option. But if they broke through, wouldn't that let the Skaridrex in?

She wanted a pause to think, but Miles pulled her down toward the dark spot in the otherwise beautiful habitat.

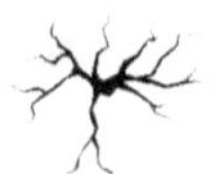

MILES FELT a slight resistance from Lira as he kicked to reach the Skaridrex intrusion, but then it stopped. She was trusting him. Should she? He wasn't sure he trusted himself. He just knew it was the only way out. They couldn't hope to break through the outer shell of the habitat expect in a spot that had been weakened.

Lira began to add her kicks to his and they moved more quickly. He reversed position and felt his feet touch down on the bottom. Lira settled next to him.

He moved her hand to his shoulder, felt her grip and then lowered himself to his knees to feel the surface. The tremor that had started above was stronger here.

He had a chilling thought. Were the Vorthari using what he'd told them to solve their Skaridrex problem? If they were, their "thank you" lacked warmth.

He rubbed his gloved hands along the darkened surface and dark pieces of material rose up into the goo, swirling in the motion possibly caused by the tremor.

If they were getting ready to flood the area around the habitat, they needed to get out now. He pulled his weapon, looked at Lira. She nodded and pulled her weapon.

Miles lifted himself just off the surface, aimed and fired. Light flashed around them as Lira fired, too.

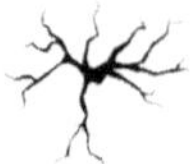

THE LIGHTS from their combined fire was too bright for Lira to see if they were having any success at breaking through. She lifted her free hand to screen her eyes and kept firing.

And then she felt the flow of the murky fluid changing. She was being pulled down in a swirling rush.

She felt Miles grip her utility belt and she spun with him into the rapidly forming vortex. She feared her suit would rip on the jagged edges of the habitat, but by some miracle the hole had widened before they got there.

Suddenly they were outside in a different kind of maelstrom. Lira couldn't process much except that Miles seemed to be trying to pull her closer to him. She kicked, trying to help him, and then his arms closed around her middle, both of his hands gripping her utility belt in the front now.

From the upward rush, they spun out into a different pulling force, one that threatened to take them back down into the habitat.

She kicked frantically now and knew Miles did, too. Her suit's sensors were pinging on every warning they possessed, at least the ones that still worked.

Her suit light still worked but it wasn't that much of

a blessing. Debris swirled in whatever substance they were now in. She took blows and knew Miles must have, too. Her suit hadn't been designed to stand up to this level of stress.

She thought Miles' head tilted back and she looked up, too.

Bubbles. The nanite bubbles were up there. They might represent safety or not.

The Skaridrex she'd seen in the arched walkway into the habitat suddenly seemed to surround them. Well, this was it, then.

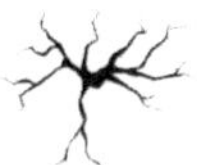

MILES THOUGHT he knew what was happening. Somehow the Vorthari had opened a vent to allow heat out and water in. It wasn't a perfect blend, which was why they weren't already dead. But the melted water was still rapidly turning eroding salt crystals into the water.

Subsidence on steroids.

Every geologist worth their salt—he winced at the unintentional joke—knew about the Lake Peigneur incident when a crew accidentally drilled into a salt mine. Water rushed into the mine, sucking the water from the lake into the mine, and taking down the drilling rig with it.

This wasn't quite the same thing, but it could be. If the water kept coming, eventually the facility over their head would be sucked down and they'd be toast.

He looked up and saw the nanite bubbles. If they could reach them, they might help. He couldn't believe he even had the thought, but desperation did strange things to a brain.

He began to kick. He couldn't let go of Lira, so all he had were his legs.

And then just out of sight of his suit light, he saw the fractal patterns he'd been told were the Skaridrex.

That couldn't be good.

But maybe it was. The downward drag eased, and they actually began to rise toward the bubble barrier. More of the fractals surrounded them and the upward surge intensified until he slammed into the barrier. Luckily his hands were hooked in Lira's utility belt, or he'd have lost his hold on her from the impact.

That was the good news.

The bad news was it felt solid on this side. How did they get through it?

He didn't realize they were sinking into the wall at first, not until he saw bubbles in his periphery vision. Something grabbed the back of his belt and pulled and they burst out into the chamber on the other side of the wall.

His first sensation was extreme relief. His second that Lira was a sturdy girl. His third…was that T'Korrin flying?

The bird was screeching loudly, flying toward their exit, then whirling around as if to herd them.

The bird was right.

"We need to get out of here," he said.

"Subsidence is happening at an accelerated rate," Harold agreed.

Miles realized that Harold was retracting some kind of grapple.

"You pulled us out."

"The nanites helped," Harold said, extending a hand to pull first Lira, then Miles to their feet.

Her father was already standing by the exit tunnel.

"We need to hurry," he said.

Lira stood staring at T'Korrin, then gave herself a shake as the bird flew into the escape tunnel and out of sight.

"The slacker," she muttered and then, as Miles grabbed her hand and pulled her into a run.

IF THE TRIP down had been tense, the trip up made that look like a walk through a mildly creepy cemetery. This was every horror and sci-fi movie black moment ever.

And that was before they got to the lift. It took all he had to step into that thing with the sides of the tunnel heaving and shedding debris from walls and ceilings. They all looked like ghosts because some powder clung to their suits.

He wrapped his arms around Lira who buried her head in his shoulder and clung back. After an endless, wracking ride, they stumbled out onto the small platform. Just to make things more exciting, it was starting to crumble at the edges.

Harold took the lead, followed by Lira's father, Lira and then Miles. It felt like all the rock hounds of hell were on his heels as they scrambled up the ancient stairs, pausing from endless time and several innumerable waits for Harold to clear away more rubble than they could squeeze past.

He helped both Lira and her father up into the basement and then Harold hoisted him up and they scrambled for the door. More debris to clear away.

Through the kitchen being attacked by flying, non-breakable items.

Lira's father took the lead outside, since he knew the quickest way out.

Running.

Dodging.

Falling.

Getting up.

Running some more.

And then the atrium was in sight.

They were around it.

They spilled out into bright light. Okay, he face-planted.

He scrambled upright, noting without happiness, that steam vents had formed all around the facility.

Lira ran toward her runner, and he followed her.

Her father and Harold scrambled into their runner.

Had the father and the robot bonded while alone?

T'Korrin came with them, still screeching its warning. It circled the runner once, then flew inside.

Miles ducked, even though he was sure the bird meant to miss him. It made a mocking sound before setting down on the deck behind Lira's seat.

Engine on.

Enough power to lift.

The ground under them was rippling and moving as if it couldn't make up its mind if it was solid or fluid.

Harold and Lira's father were in the air.

So were they.

"More altitude," Miles said, trying to snap out the order.

Below them he saw the first signs the area around the facility was beginning to collapse.

Like the round habitat below, the subsidence was circular. It surged around the building, slowly at first. Then the whole facility began to rotate. Water spouting from the ground with the released steam pressure.

A sudden waterfall formed to one side, tilting the facility to one side. More and more water surged up out of the ground. In a kind of horrifying slow motion, the facility tipped more and more to the side and then sank out of sight in a slow-moving whirlpool.

All the water that had come up out of the ground, now vanished from sight down the hole.

"Wait for it," Miles said, even though Lira hadn't made a sound.

As they circled about the now gaping hole, water began to seep upwards again. The water was probably hot, he decided because it kept bubbling up. The edges began to freeze, the ice creeping slowly toward the center of the newly formed lake.

Something appeared in that center.

The roof of the facility.

It didn't fully emerge. It bobbed up a little, then sank until just the corner of the roof was still visible, a small, dark island in a sea of mostly white ice.

"Sedimentary, my dear..." he didn't finish the sentence. He'd always wanted a reason to say it, but

Lira wasn't the right audience. It was possible there wasn't a right audience.

Following Harold's lead, Lira turned her runner until they were well away from area. They both landed and they all climbed out. Harold had picked a small ice drift that had enough rise so they could see the facility, or rather what was left of it.

"Well," Lira's father said, finally breaking the long silence, "that is a very interesting turn of events."

Even Harold turned to give him a look that Miles believed was incredulous.

Lira tried a couple of times to speak, but she ended up just shaking her head.

T'Korrin made a disgusted sound and flew up to land on top of the runner.

"You could fly all this time, couldn't you?" Lira said.

The bird ruffled his feathers in a way that looked very much like a shrug to Miles.

"He started flying because we weren't paying attention to his warning that something was very wrong," her father said. "We weren't too worried when you didn't come out, but then he got very agitated. The nanite barrier began to change colors, too."

"And the seismic activity increased," Harold put in.

"How did you know when and where to retrieve

us?" Miles asked. It wasn't need-to-know or anything, but he was curious.

"The nanites signaled me when you made contact with their surface," Harold said. "I deployed my grapple."

"Thank you," Miles said, and Lira echoed it.

If he didn't know better, he'd say the robot was embarrassed.

"Of course."

"And thank you, T'Korrin," Miles added. "I wish we could thank the nanites," he added.

"I'm sorry they are stuck in there," Lira said.

"They will be fine," Harold said.

It could have been taken as a heartless statement, but Miles had a feeling that Harold knew something they didn't. He nodded instead of asking anything more.

The bird gave the impression of a regal nod of acknowledgment.

"Is it finished, do you think?" Lira asked, turning back to gaze at what was left of the facility.

No one would be sleeping there ever again.

The ground around them was remarkably calm now.

"Finished?" Miles shook his head. "Maybe. If the chamber below filled up with water and silica, it could be relatively stable. No reason to stay here, though."

Almost reflexively, he looked up. Their ride wasn't due back for a couple more days. And what about Lira? And her father? They could fly out of here, but they'd be flying out with the knowledge that aliens had been here, both below and above ground.

For just a moment, he toyed with the idea of just disappearing into Lira's world. It didn't last. There was Harold. Miles might be able to blend, but Harold wouldn't.

"Three alien species," Lira's father murmured, as if he were just now fully realizing what it might mean.

"The Skaridrex were not a species," Harold said. "They were a defensive device created to contain the Vorthari. They had been tasked to protect humanoids. According to the nanites," he added.

"When I saw them up close, I wondered," he said. "And they helped us in there." He looked at Lira. "We were being pulled down and then we weren't."

She nodded. "I thought it was the end, but…"

Then it wasn't.

And he still had a big problem to sort out. *Don't make contact* had become *how do I handle contact until someone who knows how to do this gets here?*

"How are your people likely to deal with the knowledge they aren't alone in the universe?" Miles really didn't want to get dissected, or anything like it.

"It will be fine," Lira's father said, neither looking or sounding convinced that fine would happen.

"How did your world take it?" Lira asked.

Miles saw Harold shift its feet. It was such a human movement for a robot. Miles resisted the urge to follow its example. He probably shouldn't mention the war that broke out almost immediately upon their arrival in the Garradian Galaxy. Or their mostly paranoid movies and television shows.

"It was great," he said.

IT HADN'T BEEN hard to get Miles and Harold to her place without them being spotted as aliens.

Aliens.

Now that she was back in her own place, her own part of the world, she had time to wrap her brain around the whole alien thing and feel the shock of it to her toenails. She'd felt herself starting to shut down when they'd successfully escaped the facility. She'd caught Miles glancing at her from time to time, but to her relief he hadn't said much.

She'd listened to him talking to her father about what could happen, if her people wanted off-world contact. And if they didn't want it?

Then Miles would go away.

He'd been very clear that these Garradians weren't into conquest. They liked meeting people and learning about them.

And they'd helped them eons ago when the Vorthari had first arrived.

Arrived?

Her suit had recorded a lot of the Vorthari story, and she'd had time to study it. Now she was sure that what they'd actually done was attack their planet. And they'd been trying to escape from the Skaridrex, which —aided by the nanites, had protected them.

But even her father admitted their story was going to be a hard sell to their leaders. Other than the video from her suit, she had no physical evidence. There was that abandoned dig. It might become important now.

But Miles might still go away.

She tried to ignore the twist of her heart at this thought. Of course, she liked him. He'd saved her life down there. If he'd let go of her, well, she couldn't think about it without a shudder.

She gave herself a shake and tried to focus on her video. It was unsettling to watch it, to relive it all. But then her thoughts focused sharply on something she'd forgotten in the chaos of trying to escape.

There were others.

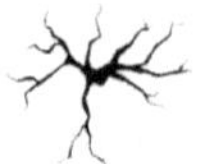

MILES' ride had come, complained mightily, and left. It would be back, either with a delegation or some military police to arrest him.

He would have liked to stay if they sent a delegation. It was a nice planet for a geologist. It had a lot of rocks, and all that seismic activity? It was sweet.

Lira's place, where he and Harold were temporarily guesting, was like her. Practical, with touches of girly stuff. It was, she'd told him, unusual for a housing pad to be this isolated but she liked the seclusion when she was working. It had been a huge bonus for them, since the level of nosy neighbors was almost zero.

He'd have liked to go out and explore a little, but every time he made a move for the door, he found Harold on his heels. It was, he supposed, classic sidekick behavior, or it had been ordered to keep him under wraps until the delegation could get here.

His glance strayed to Lira, working on her version of a computer.

She was as sweet as all the geology on her planet.

He knew some from the Expedition and some of the others had brought back aliens, but Lira, well, this was her home. She had family here, brothers in addition to her father. She had a life, a purpose, a career here.

And they'd known each other for about a week.

If he were honest with himself, he'd wondered if he'd ever find a girl that was more interesting than rocks. Apparently, he'd just been in the wrong galaxy for that.

He stopped glancing at her and just looked, noting all the things he liked about her.

Of course, she was nice to look at, great to kiss. But he'd been through the fire—or the raging water—with her. She'd gone down into that pit to find her father. She'd gone into the habitat to find the truth, to help. If she'd been half as scared as he'd have been?

She was definitely a keeper.

A keeper he wasn't supposed to meet or keep.

He was in so much trouble.

Lira spun around in her seat, her eyes wide.

"We might still have a Vorthari problem," she said.

He probably shouldn't have found that kind of hopeful to hear. He rose from his seat and crossed to her.

She spun around, thinking maybe that he wanted to see what she'd found. He didn't, but he looked anyway. He even kind of listened. But what he heard?

He might be able to stay long enough to…

"Lira," he said.

Maybe something in his voice jerked her out of her Vorthari absorption. She looked up at him.

He held out his hand to her, holding his breath as he waited for her to take it. Or not. Probably not…

She took it, let him pull her up from her seat.

She let him slide his arms around her waist and pull her gently, carefully close. He inhaled the sweet, vaguely foreign scent of her.

"How does a guy from another planet court a girl from yours?"

She lifted her head, her eyes soft and glowing. "Court?"

"Spend time with intent to spend," he swallowed as fear almost choked off the words, "the rest of his life with her."

"Court." This time she said the word with a different inflection. "Won't they make you leave?"

"They aren't like that," he said. "We don't make people do things, at least, I'm not military. I could stay."

"For always?"

"If that's what you want," he said. The fear tried to choke him again. "If that's what you want." The words sounded stronger this time. How did he feel about living here forever? He wasn't sure. He just knew he wanted to be with Lira.

"What if," her gaze dropped now, "I wanted to see your world?"

"That," he swallowed dryly, "could probably be arranged."

Her lips curved up in a smile that stole his breath and his heart—okay, she'd already stolen that, but the smile solidified the deal.

He bent his head, his lips finding hers. And he knew that wherever they were, she was his world now.

ONE LAST THING...

Thank you for taking this journey with *Claws & Effect.*

I hope the adventures stayed with you long after the final page — the danger, the connection, and that feeling of everything clicking into place at the end.

Read Next:

If you'd like to see where the *Project Enterprise* journey began, here's the main series in order:

The Key (book 1)

Girl Gone Nova (book 2)

Tangled in Time (book 3)

Steamrolled (book 4)

Kicking Ashe (book 5)

The Reboot Books of Project Enterprise

Found Girl (book 6)

Lost Valyr (book 7)

Maestra Rising (book 8)

Each book builds on the last, expanding the universe, the relationships, and the stakes.

About the Project Enterprise Series

Project Enterprise is a romantic science-fiction adventure series about courage under pressure, unexpected connection, and finding your footing when the universe refuses to play fair.

Fast-paced missions, time-bending twists, and hopeful endings — because even after the wildest ride, some things are worth fighting for.

Already Read Project Enterprise Series? The Adventures continue in the Spin-off series: The Cyborg Chronicles

Cyborg's Revenge: The Cyborg Chronicles Book 1

Cosmic Boom: The Cyborg Chronicles Book 2

CabeX: The Cyborg Chronicles Book 3

AzumC: The Cyborg Chronicles Book 4

MircoP: The Cyborg Chronicles Book 5

ScytheQ: The Cyborg Chronicles 6

OmnitronW: The Cyborg Chronicles 7

TalusH: The Cyborg Chronicles 8 (coming in 2026)

TrackerY: The Cyborg Chronicles 9 (coming in 2027)

Find Out What Happens After

She trusted the cyborg. Can she trust the man?

Tim was once an unstoppable cyborg. Now he's human again—too human, with a body that feels clumsy, emotions he doesn't know how to control, and one scientist he can't get out of his system.

Riina Katala never expected her friendship with Tim to turn into something that keeps her awake at night. But seeing him in his new, flesh-and-blood form stirs feelings she's not ready to face—especially when duty demands she lead a dangerous mission with him at her side.

Their task? Rescue a stranded geologist before his accidental first contact ignites a planetary disaster.

Their risk? Facing the truth about each other while

an ominous alien presence darkens the skies above Arroxan Prime.

Caught between duty and desire, Tim and Riina must decide if they can be more than partners—or if the universe has other plans.

From award-winning author Pauline Baird Jones comes a perilously fun, heart-pounding space adventure of love, loyalty, and second chances.

Prologue

Dr. Miles Walker still wasn't sure how his mission to Arroxan Prime had ended up going sideways. He probably should have realized that an Earth geology degree wasn't that much help on another planet, in a whole other galaxy.

But he had tried to follow his orders, but he was a geologist, not a diplomat. It wasn't his fault that *don't make contact* had become *how do I handle contact until someone who knows how to do this first contact thing gets here?*

It had all seemed to simple before he got here. Discover why a millenniums old sensor had turned on, and if possible, turn it off. The only reason he'd been chosen for the mission was because the sensor registered seismic disruptions. The connection between a sensor malfunction and earthquakes was a little thin, but he'd figured they hadn't had anyone else to send.

He'd done what he could to solve the problem but under the heading of "expect the unexpected," his solution might have triggered more problems. Oops. So here he was, stuck on a distant planet, trying to diplomat without starting a war.

Luckily there was an upside.

Miles looked at the upside—Lira Taan—with what he hoped was a serious and thoughtful expression, one minus the utter terror he felt about possibly screwing things up even more. Or getting dissected as an alien.

"How are your people likely to deal with the knowledge they aren't alone in the universe?" Miles asked.

"It will be fine," Lira's father said, neither looking or sounding convinced that fine would happen.

"How did your world take it?" Lira asked.

Her level of confidence in him was as unsettling as her eyes, her lips, her—he gave himself a shake. So far neither Lira or her father had stated that dissection was off the table. He needed to focus.

Miles noticed Harold shift its feet. It was such a human movement for a robot. Miles resisted the urge to follow its example. He probably shouldn't mention the war that broke out almost immediately upon their Expedition's arrival in the Garradian Galaxy. Or their mostly paranoid movies and television shows.

"It was great," he said. "A real party."

POLLIN SOLLIN ALMOST MISSED IT. He was just pushing back his chair when his equipment registered…something.

He stared at the signal. He'd seen the same thing a few days ago. Was it, could it be, a communication signal?

It matched nothing in his database that was associated with Arroxan Prime's standard communications. Could it be…an off-world communication?

He tried to tamp down the surge of hope. He'd been here before. He'd seen what could be communication signals broadcasting at a range not used even by their military. And he had been disappointed time and again.

But....even the signals he broadcast in hopes of reaching something, or someone, weren't at the range this one registered on his equipment.

He hesitated, then settled back down in front of his broadcasting equipment and dialed his signal up. His finger hovered over the command to send it out into the cosmos. He wasn't supposed to use it. It was dangerous. It was reckless. It was—he pressed it.

Chapter 1

Riina Katala stood in the shadows watching Tim—formerly an OmnitronW robot—talking to his physical therapist.

She didn't remember what she'd thought he'd look like. The reality had wiped away all expectations and left her…winded…every time she saw him.

It was disconcerting.

From imposing and towering lethal metal to *this*.

Oh, he had retained his lethal aura, and he still exuded extreme competence. But now it was all packaged into tall, broad, muscled, and *human.* So potently human.

Had she known he had been this good-looking would she have encouraged him to return to his cloned human body? And how had he left this behind? Hadn't he realized…but of course, it hadn't mattered. He'd been a slave of the *Q'uy*.

It wasn't as if he'd had a choice. But, as she often heard the Earth humans say, "Dang, he was pretty."

They'd been friends almost from their first meeting. They had done multiple diplomatic missions together, including the very dangerous one with General Halliwell.

Despite his lethal appearance, she'd felt completely safe with him.

What did she feel now?

Not something that felt safe, that was for sure.

Why did her heart hammer in her chest when she saw him? Why did her face feel hot, and her hands feel cold?

She needed to figure this out before they came face-to-face again. Before they had to leave for their next mission.

She'd dreamt about him last night. She'd been in the hangar bay waiting for him, just like so many times before. The door had slid back and he'd stepped through it. Not the robot. The man.

Their eyes—his human eye—had found her and she'd rocked back on her heels. There'd been a question in there, and he'd held out his hand to her. She'd walked to him, surprised to find she could move.

Surprised at how eager she'd been to take his outstretched hand.

His so very human hand had closed around hers and she'd been flooded with a feeling that felt so right that tears had pricked her dream eyes.

She'd woken up shaken and disoriented to find herself alone. She'd flexed the hand he'd held, still feeling the tingle in her skin from the dream contact.

She had thrown back her coverings and gone to get water to drink. It had helped. A little. She'd leaned her head against the cold wall, trying to regain her composure.

Riina was a scientist and she'd always prided herself on her command of her emotions—both before their long sleep and now in this unsettling future she'd landed in.

She liked Tim, the cyborg. Her mind and his had… meshed. They'd made a good team. He could both think logically and break things when things needed to be broken. A smile had flickered on her lips at this thought. She had been mildly infected with the way the people of the Earth Expedition talked.

She should have realized she might have caught other things from them. They were a people who were unabashed about who they were and what they felt a situation required. Their belief in themselves extended from breaking things to, well, romance.

She was sincerely happy for those of her kind who had found happiness with those from the Earth Expedition and others of the former cyborgs. She just didn't know how to reconcile who she'd believed she was and this…surge of emotion that had been infiltrating her mind even before Tim made the decision to migrate from mostly robotic cyborg to mostly human cyborg.

And then there was the other factor.

Tim.

What did he think? What did he feel?

Just because she'd lost her mind, didn't mean he had. Just because he met her halfway in her dreams didn't mean he would when he was released from medical and cleared to return to duty.

Duty.

What did duty dictate for either of them?

She wasn't new to fear. Fear had sent them into their long sleep. But this fear, which was obviously less life threatening, felt worse than that fear.

Why?

Tim lifted a towel to his glistening face and rubbed it, his body turning in her direction. She stepped back quickly, then slipped away, afraid of what she'd see in his eyes when he saw her.

And afraid of what she wouldn't see.

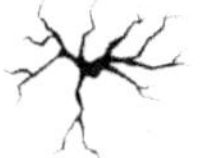

"WE HAVE A PROBLEM," Delilah "Doc" Clementyne avoided looking at General Halliwell as she began the process of delivering this new round of bad news. She couldn't even play the good news, bad news card. So far, there was no good news card in her deck.

In the wall's reflection, she saw him turn around. And she heard his sigh.

"What now?"

"Do you remember that geologist the Garradians borrowed?"

There was a short silence. He was pretending to think, but she knew he didn't need to. He had every person's name they'd loaned to the Garradians on mental speed dial.

"Dr. Walker." Another pause. "Dr. Miles Walker. What did he do? Oh wait. Let me guess. He made first contact."

"It was probably a given," Doc said. It was an unexpected that she'd pretty much expected. So technically, not unexpected. "There seems to be a woman in the mix."

She knew the general wanted to rant about it, but it was difficult for him. He'd gone on a mission and come back involved with an alien. It was also almost a given that anyone who went out on an expedition came back in love with an alien.

She cast a quick glance at her alien. Hel grinned.

None of them had a leg to stand on.

"Do we have a solution?" Halliwell asked.

"Well, we have to form a mission to try to contain the fallout. The Maestra has suggested Riina Katala and Tim." Doc once again kept her tone carefully neutral.

Dr. Miles Walker was one of theirs and neither Riina or Tim were part of the Expedition. But they had done a mission with the General. He knew them both very well and respected them.

Now the General did look around. Doc warily turned to face him.

"Is Tim out of medical?"

"Yes, and he is finishing up his physical therapy." Tim, a former robot with a human consciousness, had recently transferred that consciousness back into a body cloned from his own DNA.

She had to give their ship's captain, CabeX, kudos for forward thinking. Back when the robots had left their human bodies, he'd foreseen a time when they might want to go back to their original forms and saved their DNA.

Not all of them had ended up back in their own

cloned bodies, however. Necessity had required different outcomes for some of them. But Tim was back in a version of his own body.

That should have meant an easy integration, but apparently living for years in a robot body required a lot of adjustment when leaving the big, bad robot body behind.

She wasn't unsympathetic. She'd had to make some big adjustments since coming to the Garradian Galaxy—the biggest one being Helfron Giddioni.

She might still be trying to get used to his name. And having an alien and hostile mother-in-law. And becoming a step-mom to two little Giddionis. And…the nanites living inside her…well, a lot of adjustments to new things.

Hel's lips quirked up as if he knew what she was thinking. He probably did. They were connected in ways that was yet another of those adjustments.

"Other than Dr. Miles being our guy, what does this have to do with me?" Halliwell rubbed his face.

"The Maestra wanted you to be informed, in case you wanted to embed one of your people in the mission."

The general sighed again. "I, yes, I do. Let me think about who to send." He glanced up in time to catch her slight grimace. "Not a diplomat."

Yes, they both still had issues with diplomats.

"Thank you, sir." She knew how to look demure when needed and she deployed the look now.

The general snorted. "Dismissed, Doc."

"Yes, sir."

It wasn't an oversight that he never acknowledged Hel unless forced to by circumstances. The general knew how to hold a grudge.

Hel waited until they were safely outside to laugh.

"Do you think he'll task himself…" Hel began.

"No, he won't," Doc told him. "He'll want to, but he won't."

She meshed her fingers with his and saw the heat spark in his eyes. The general and his issues faded from her mind. And Doc was pretty sure they faded from Hel's too.

TIM FOLLOWED CabeX into the meeting room. Trac—TrackerY—came in last and stopped near the door. The robotic cyborg couldn't show unease, but Tim knew Trac well enough to know how much Trac didn't want to be in this room with them.

Tim hadn't asked CabeX why he'd detailed Trac to the mission—partly because Tim didn't know what the mission was. And CabeX always had his reasons for what he did. His crew had learned to just follow orders.

The Garradian Maestra was already in the room. It was not a surprise to see Moose—also a former cyborg—at her back, since they were a couple.

She smiled a greeting, then gave CabeX a puzzled look.

"I don't believe I've met…" she didn't finish the sentence, just indicated Trac with a wave of her hand.

It was true that as cybernetic robots, the *Najer* crew weren't that different in appearance—to others—at first. But each of them had been specific models with special functions, over and above their basic intimidation factors. And as these people came to know them, they'd gradually been able to discern the differences in their various models.

And now only two of them remained in robot form, so it should be a lot easier. But it was also true that Trac didn't get out a lot. Tim wasn't sure he'd been off the ship at all since they started working with the Expedition and the Garradians.

"This is TrackerY," CabeX said. "Trac," he added.

"Trac. Pleased to meet you." She still looked puzzled.

Trac inclined his head, his hands folded across his massive, metal chest.

"Ma'am," he said. His voice was the most robotic of the crew's.

Tim had always figured it was a personal choice.

"He doesn't leave the *Najer* that often," CabeX said.

"Okay." The Maestra blinked a couple of times, gave a slight head shake, then gestured for them to take seats.

All of them but Trac did. He stayed near the door as the Maestra began to explain the problem unfolding on Arroxan Prime.

Tim might be surprised he was being tasked with the mission. It sounded like a diplomatic problem. None of the crew off the *Najer* were particularly good at that. Breaking things. Shooting things. Hacking into things. Yes. Talking nice? No.

"Who else is on the mission?" Tim finally asked. Surely someone from the Earth Expedition was going, since it was their guy in trouble. Or possibly in trouble. They didn't seem quite sure about that yet.

A list appeared on a screen in front of them. The only name Tim saw was Riina Katala. His newly human body reacted strongly, his heartbeat speeding up. And other parts felt strange and alien. *Riina.*

He hadn't seen her since he'd gone into medical for his consciousness transfer. He'd half hoped she'd come to see him, been mostly relieved she hadn't. He hadn't liked feeling so much less as he fought to recover from the transfer and accustom himself to a mostly human body.

He didn't know how to feel or act around her from inside this body.

He might be glad the choice had been removed. Now he'd have to see her.

"I'm conflicted about sending one person so obviously alien," the Maestra admitted, her glance flicking to Tim.

He did have obvious cybernetics. Like some of the others, he'd been reluctant to completely live without cybernetics.

"They don't have…" CabeX stopped as if unsure how to phrase the question.

Tim couldn't help him out.

"From what we can tell, no, but we're going in as alien anyway. And there is a bigger problem than just accidental first contact," she admitted.

A report popped up on his personal screen. It took him longer to absorb it than he was used to, but he still looked up before CabeX.

CabeX had gone fully human.

"Interesting," he said.

"Can I bring my my Skitterfin?" Trac asked. "My pet."

They all turned to look at him.

Trac had a pet?

Tim looked at CabeX who gave a shrug.

"Sure."

CabeX didn't sound sure, but if it got Trac out and about…

"Sure," Tim echoed. What was a skitterfin?

Chapter 2

"Our passengers are entering the flight deck, Captain."

Captain Nevv Kellen looked up from his control deck. Veirn, the *Quendala's* onboard AI, was broadcasting video from the flight deck.

Kellen had studied their information packets, supplied to him by the Maestra, but this was his first time getting eyes on some of them. He'd flown missions with Riina and Tim before, though this was a new Tim, a mostly human Tim. Or somewhat human Tim? Only time would answer that question.

The TrackerY robot, Trac, was a disturbing sight with the three-tailed skitterfin on his shoulder. Its three tails wrapped his cyborg head and its wings were tucked in.

Nevv had never liked skitterfens. As a general rule he didn't like any animals on his ship. They were difficult to control and often acted on impulse. Its inclusion in the mission had been done without his input.

He studied the female soldier walking behind Trac. Her name was Lt. Lovely Dish, so he'd expected her to be anything but lovely. He wasn't sorry to be wrong.

He'd noticed when anyone mentioned Lieutenant Dish, the men fell silent. Now he knew why.

She was blonde, generously built, and her walk might have stalled his thinking for several seconds. Or longer.

It was a small team, but Arroxan Prime wasn't a high priority contact planet, being situated off the beaten flight paths and isolated in their little system. He'd studied the system, too, and had mentally labeled it as mostly dysfunctional. It had only one slightly habitable planet. How had anyone found their way there?

They were only sending the mission because contact had happened, not because any of them wanted to make contact with the planet's inhabitants.

From his perusal of the mission report, Dr. Miles Walker had gone to investigate a seismic warning sensor and tripped over everything in sight. And several things not in sight.

At least he seemed to realize it. He'd been deployed with a robot assist module named Harold—there had to be a story there—but even it couldn't save Dr. Walker from himself. Or from first contact.

On the good news side of the equation, the contact was limited so far. Nothing official yet.

They'd have probably just pulled Dr. Walker and Harold out, but the problem that had triggered the sensor seemed to be systemic and possibly planet-wide.

Current protocol was to interfere as little as possible in a planet's affairs, but back before the long sleep? A lot of interfering had occurred, with Arroxan Prime as a, well, prime example. He wasn't clear on the nature of the interference, but if sensors had been planted? Interfering had occurred.

There was a short delay at the boarding ramp, as man and robot signaled for the two women to board first. Riina didn't hesitate, but Lt. Dish engaged in a short argument with Tim before giving in and coming aboard.

With some reluctance, he stood, smoothing down his uniform before turning and striding to the hatch. It was time to welcome the team aboard.

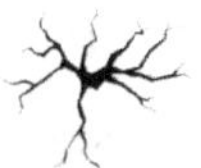

RIINA LED the way to the *Quendala's* lounge. Even if she hadn't been aboard this ship before, its design was similar to others of its type that had been brought back into service as more and more of them woke from the long sleep. It helped to lead their small group. This meant she didn't have to look at Tim yet. They'd exchanged greetings at the hatch, of course, but somehow their glances hadn't intersected.

As she walked down the main corridor, she tried to ignore the tingling sensations traveling up and down her back. It was probably her imagination that Tim stared at her. That and wishful thinking? She pushed that thought away as firmly as she could manage.

From the opposite direction, the captain, Nevv Kellen approached, lifting a hand in greeting.

She was pleased to be traveling with him once more. He had a steady head in a crisis and was also brave and resourceful. The ship's AI, Veirn, had an interesting sense of humor, but personality quirks seemed to be the order of the day as more and more of the Garradian assets were assembled and reactivated.

"Captain," she said, giving him a respectful nod, before smiling and holding out her hand.

He took her hand, but his attention shifted past her. Either to Lt. Dish or the team in general, she wasn't sure. Well, she might suspect it was Lt. Dish. She seemed to have an interesting effect on the men.

"Small team this time," Kellen noted. "Optimism or…"

"Caution," Riina finished. They weren't exactly expecting things to go badly, but Arroxan Prime was a planet that did not appear to have indulged in any type of star ward looking. And, between experience and time spent in Doc's company, Riina was learning to expect the unexpected. And the worst from the unexpected.

It was entirely possible the populace would become a little agitated at the realization that first contact had happened. Or a lot. Full on panic was also on what Doc liked to call the Bingo card, whatever that meant. And they might reject any attempts to help them with their Vorthari infestation.

There was the video from Dr. Walker's contact, but would they believe it? The Vorthari were unusual appearing aliens. Unsettling but also beautiful. The aliens, the Skaridrex, who'd helped contain the Vorthari at the initial contact site were not beautiful. That might be a problem.

Multiple Garradian scientific teams had studied the data transmitted from Dr. Walker's encounter with the Vorthari. They hoped to discover their origins and why they'd migrated to Arroxan Prime. They were all certain they weren't natural to the planet. She wasn't sure why yet.

There was one theory currently being discussed that the Vorthari were the source of the extreme volcanic activity the planet experienced. Did that mean the Vorthari predated the human occupants?

Anything was possible which was just another way of saying, "expect the unexpected."

"We have contact with Dr. Walker and Harold," Riina continued. So far everything he'd supplied indicated a people who weren't that interested in the stars. Even their alien conspiracy theories seemed to be focused underground.

And they weren't wrong about that.

There was a short pause, then the captain cleared his throat.

"You'll each find a path customized to your ID that will lead you to your quarters. We'll be lifting off shortly. Locate your secure seating for both lift-off and when we activate the star drive or you'll have some unpleasant moments."

They had to be well clear of the outpost before they could activate the star drive, Riina knew.

"Thank you, Captain," Riina said. She glanced at her timepiece. "Let's return here in half an hour? We have some video from Dr. Walker to study. It's from their entertainment broadcasts. We need to get a feel for the inhabitants of Arroxan Prime."

"Cool," Lt. Dish said. She bent to pick up her gear, but Trac beat her—and Tim—to it.

"Let me assist you," Trac said. "I have no gear to stow."

Now Tim turned toward her, but it felt as if he avoided her gaze.

"You brought no gear?" he asked.

"I brought it aboard earlier," Riina said. She and the captain had needed to discuss their approach to the planet.

Was it her imagination that Tim's gaze shot toward the captain for a few seconds?

She gave an imperceptible sigh. This mission was going to be challenging on multiple levels.

Chapter 3

Pollin Sollin walked quickly down the quiet street, stopping at intervals to check his surroundings. And once he stopped for a particularly troublesome tremor. Their leaders claimed the seismic activity wasn't getting worse, but Pollin wasn't sure he believed them.

He stopped in front of a two-story house—none of their buildings were particularly tall—glanced both ways and then slipped up to the door, using the shadows of the low-lying bushes in the yard as much as possible.

He gave the knock. Listened for the return knock. Knocked again.

The door opened just enough for him to slip inside. A blanket hung over the door, so that no light could escape into the street. The windows had been blacked out, too.

Despite these precautions, the lighting was dim, the shapes around the room shadowy.

Any other night, the precautions would have amused him.

He knew everyone there. And they knew him. There'd been no new members since Herk Taan had relocated to the southern pole.

He had been a good recruiter, too good some thought.

It wasn't that their gathering was illegal. Their government was indifferent to their cause. But sometimes employers were less willing to overlook their level of interest in alien life forms.

"Has anyone heard from Herk?" Drun Marik was their unofficial head. He had to be particularly careful because he worked for state security.

His bosses probably knew what Drun got up to in his spare time, but he was good at his job and what was the harm?

Pollin took an empty seat at the back. He wasn't sure, but he thought he was the last one there. He'd debated coming. He sat with his hands clenched in his lap, his fist clenching and unclenching.

At first, he'd been so excited. This was what they'd been waiting for, searching for, planning for.

But was *this* that?

He touched the data sheet tucked in his jacket's inside pocket.

Two signals. He'd identified two signals. He'd confirmed two signals.

One planet based.

And one space based.

He wasn't wrong.

He wanted to be wrong.

Only he wasn't.

It wasn't as if signals of this type could be faked.

He was almost one hundred percent sure they couldn't be faked.

He knew one person who would know if Pollin had stumbled into something governmental, something that would be illegal to know about.

Drun would know. But if he knew, why hadn't he said something or at least hinted at it?

Was it because one of the signals was space based? Had the government finally turned their attention to the stars?

There were so few of them who looked up, even in their group. From the time they learned to walk, his people looked down. It was the only way to keep from falling when a tremor hit.

If one was star gazing, one would soon be face planting.

"Any new business?" Drun asked.

Pollin realized he'd missed all the old business while lost in his thoughts. He took a steadying breath. It was now or never.

He lifted his hand, glad the light was too bad for anyone to see the tremble. Then he rose.

"I have," he hesitated, not sure what to call it, "information."

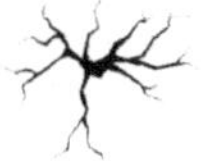

PROJECT ENTERPRISE: **The Cyborg Chronicles**

In the far reaches of the Garradian galaxy, survival comes at a price.

Forged through war, experimentation, and loss, the men and women of Project Enterprise are more than human — and more than machine. As cyborg operatives aboard the starship *Najer*, they face deadly missions, ruthless enemies, and impossible odds… while searching for something no technology can replace: their humanity.

Each story delivers high-stakes action, fast-paced adventure, and a closed-door romantic arc where trust, loyalty, and connection grow amid chaos. With humor threaded through danger and hope rising from the ashes of conflict, **The Cyborg Chronicles** is a sweeping sci-fi romance series about reclaiming choice, identity, and love among the stars.

Adventure awaits. The galaxy is watching.

Continue the Adventure

If you enjoyed this journey through the Garradian galaxy, the story continues in the next book of **The Cyborg Chronicles**.

Read OmnitronW To Find Out What Happens to Miles and Riina:

OmnitronW: The Cyborg Chronicles 7

New dangers. New missions. And another cyborg fighting for his future — and his heart.

Thank You for Reading

I'm so glad you took time to check out the crew of the *Najer*.

I hope you'll continue the adventure — the galaxy still has many secrets to reveal.

— Pauline Baird Jones

Books by Pauline Baird Jones

Science Fiction Romance/Paranormal

Project Enterprise: The Cyborg Chronicles

Cyborg's Revenge: The Cyborg Chronicles Book 1
Cosmic Boom: The Cyborg Chronicles Book 2
CabeX: The Cyborg Chronicles Book 3
AzumC: The Cyborg Chronicles Book 4
MircoP: The Cyborg Chronicles Book 5
ScytheQ: The Cyborg Chronicles 6
OmnitronW: The Cyborg Chronicles 7
TalusH: The Cyborg Chronicles 8
TrackerY: The Cyborg Chronicles 9

Project Universe Series:

The Key (book 1)
Girl Gone Nova (book 2)

Tangled in Time (book 3)

Steamrolled (book 4)

Kicking Ashe (book 5)

The Reboot Books of Project Enterprise

Found Girl (book 6)

Lost Valyr (book 7)

Maestra Rising (book 8)

More Project Enterprise

Project Enterprise: The Short Stories

Time Trap: A Project Enterprise Series Short Story

Operation Ark: A Project Enterprise Story

General's Holiday: A Project Enterprise Story

Claws & Effect: The Otherworldly Pets of Project Enterprise

Echoes Beneath: A Project Enterprise Story (included in Pets in Space 10)

Other Romantic Science Fiction Stories

The Real Dragon

Nebula Nine (time travel adventure)

Open With Care (Christmas collection that includes, "Riding For Christmas" and "Up on the House Top"

Specters in the Storm: A paranormal/steampunk/science fiction romance novella

Out of Time Series (Award-winning Romantic Time Travel):

Out of Time
Just in Time
Telling Time
Out of Time Series (Three Book Bundle)

An Uneasy Future

(A science fiction romance mystery series set in future New Orleans)

Core Punch (1.0)
Sucker Punch (2.0)
One Two Punch: An Uneasy Future Bundle

Romantic Suspense

The Big Uneasy Series:

Relatively Risky (1)
Family Treed (A Big Uneasy Short Story)
Dead Spaces (2.0)
Louisiana Lagniappe (3.0)
Worry Beads (4.0)
Fais Do Do Die (5.0)
Beaucoup Fracas (6.0)
Pirogue Wipe Out (7.0)
Bourre Brouhaha (8.0)
Soc Au' Lait Stiff (9.0)
The Family Way (A Big Uneasy Short Story)
Guess Who's Coming To Christmas: The Wedding Edition

The Big Uneasy Bundle

An Uneasy Collection: The Big Uneasy Books 3-5

Lonesome Lawmen Series:

The Last Enemy

Byte Me

Missing You

Lonesome Mama (Bonus short story)

(The *Lonesome Lawmen* is also available as a digital bundle)

Do Wah Diddy Die

The Spy Who Kissed Me

*Perilously Fun Fiction Bundle (*includes *The Spy Who Kissed Me* and *Do Wah Diddy Die.* Bonus: *Do Wah Diddy Delete Short Story Collection)*

Dangerous Dance

Dangerous Duet

Short Story Collections

Project Enterprise: The Short Stories

Do Wah Diddy Delete

Let's Fall in Love

The Real Dragon and other short stories

About the Author

Award-winning author Pauline Baird Jones writes *perilously fun fiction*—from romantic suspense to space opera, time travel and more. With 40+ books, a flair for humor, and a love of adventure, she creates heroines braver than they realize and heroes brave enough to love them. If you crave thrilling plots, smart laughs, and happy endings, you're in the right place! 🚀💚📚

To find out more about Pauline or her books:

http://paulinebjones.com

www.ingramcontent.com/pod-product-compliance
Lightning Source LLC
LaVergne TN
LVHW010916110826
845149LV00013B/2379